NEWSPAPER BOY

A SHORT NOVEL WITH LONG CHAPTERS

MARK MACGOUGAN

ISBN: 1540593029
ISBN-13: 978-1540593023

In loving memory of Meg, Princess of the Glenwood Gazette.

Cover photograph by Laura MacGougan.

No animals were harmed in the writing of this book.

CONTENTS

1. THE CHURCH FLOWER LADY OF WORDS ON A DEADLINE

There's a stretch of Thomson Road that used to be a community swimming pool. Now there are a couple of houses there that don't quite fit with the other houses in the neighborhood. This is one of the complications of getting older. You remember what used to be somewhere. I see 23 and 25 Thomson and I think of the missing pool.

I suppose grown-ups must see missing swimming pools all over the place. I'm eleven, and it's a fairly new experience for me. I used to take things more at face value. Back say when I was in single digits, pretty much everything seemed equally new to me. Or maybe equally old.

My older brother and I operate a newspaper in our neighborhood. His name is Brian, the neighborhood is called Thomson Acres and the newspaper is called the Thomson Acres Tribune. We debated calling it the Thomson Acres No-Pee Gazette in honor of the no-p spelling of Thomson. That would have been a pretty funny name and maybe we should have used it, but we didn't want people to think the newspaper was a joke. It would be enough of a challenge to have people take us seriously without giving the paper a goofy name. So it's the Thomson Acres Tribune.

We publish the paper weekly when we can, which works out to about three times a month. We print up a run of about 100 copies on Friday night, although we never sell them out. Over the weekend, we visit the houses in the neighborhood, selling the papers and getting news for the next issue.

We do this thing Old School. The paper is only available hard copy. We don't have a website or a Facebook page or a Twitter account. The paper has an email address that people can use to send in news items, but that's it. You want our news, you buy a hard copy paper. In theory you can subscribe, but mostly we just sell individual copies as they come out. Dad says it's better that way. The more people we talk to, the more we'll know about what's happening in the neighborhood. Of course, Dad isn't the one walking around ringing everybody's doorbell.

Being Old School, I make my weekend rounds wearing a sports coat. I have a dual role of newspaper delivery and reporter, and the sports coat helps to emphasize the reporter side of the job.

My sports coat has inside pockets that are good for my notepad and my pod. I use my pod to record interviews and take pictures. It looks like a smartphone and does about everything a smartphone can do, only it isn't a phone. Most of my friends have smartphones of one kind or another, but I have something that looks like a phone.

I tried to reason with my parents. "What if I get kidnapped by terrorists?" I said.

They were unmoved.

"Ask to borrow a phone," said Mom.

"That's the whole point," said Dad. "You have a phone and get kidnapped by international terrorists – just think of the roaming charges!"

I'm tempted sometimes to pull out my pod and pretend to be having a phone conversation with someone. That would be bogus. I'll admit, however, that sometimes I listen to music on my pod by holding it to my ear and, if I really like the music, I might say things like "Yeah, yeah" while listening to it.

My normal Saturday route covers Thomson, Glenbrook and Springbrook roads, each of which has about fifteen houses. We live on Glenbrook, but I like to go out to the end of Springbrook and work my way back. Especially as I'm getting started, it's easier to think of myself as a journalist when I'm not within sight of my own house.

When I was young, Mom would come with me on my rounds. She was actually pretty good about it. She'd wait by the street like it was Halloween and she didn't want to hover too much. She'd wave back to anyone who waved at her, but that was it. Then one day I guess she decided it was safe enough or I was old enough, and I've been doing it on my own ever since.

Thomson Acres is a good area for a neighborhood newspaper. It's not too big for us to cover. It's safe enough that Mom lets us go around and knock on everybody's door, but it's not so posh that you have to walk a football field between one house and another.

From a distance, all the houses tend to look alike. When you get close, you see the differences. My first house, at the very end of Springbrook (#36, the DiFurias), is perfect. Peek in the windows and it looks like a house in a magazine. Mr. DiFuria is a nut about his lawn. Nice people, though, and good customers.

I ring the bell. The DiFuria bell has a deep, two-tone gong sound, easily heard as you ring it. I like that. I hate it when you push a doorbell and can't tell whether or not it works. How long should I wait before trying again or knocking? If the bell works and I keep pushing it, people are going to think I'm obnoxious. On the other hand, I've got a lot of houses to visit and can't spend all day standing around on any one porch.

Mr. DiFuria answers the door. I like Mr. DiFuria, but I'm still disappointed that it isn't Mrs. DiFuria, who is nice to me and very pretty for a grown-up. I didn't used to find grown-ups attractive in that way, so I'm thinking that's part of the territory now that I'm solidly into double figures. Brian, my brother, asked me recently what girls I liked and I named a couple. He asked me about Becca Hennessey, a girl in my class that I hadn't named and hadn't really thought about before. He said I should think about her because her Mom is hot and most girls end up growing up to look like their Moms. That makes some sense to me, but here's the thing. Last month, we had Special Friends Day at school, and Becca brought her grandmother, who isn't hot. Maybe when I'm in triple figures I'll think that Becca's grandmother is hot. So now, when I think about Becca, I think about her growing up to look like her grandma.

I don't know what I'll grow up to look like. Mom's friends sometimes say things like, "Oh, he's going to break some hearts when he gets a little older!" That's supposed to be a compliment, but it's a pretty strange one. Who wants to break anyone's heart?

Maybe I won't grow up. I seem to be lagging behind a little. A lot of my classmates are starting to look like teenagers and I still look like a kid. Don't get me wrong – I'm not in any hurry to be a teenager. Most teenagers seem to be a little brain damaged. Still, I do want people to take me seriously. Mom says I'll be glad to be young-looking when I get to be old. Maybe so. On the other hand, you know, I'll be old.

Mr. DiFuria opens the door all the way and lets go of it. This is unusual. Most people open the door halfway and peek around it, like they're afraid I'm trying to bust into their house. He's wearing work clothes, but somehow looks like he's on his way to a work clothes dinner party. "We'll take a paper!" he says, handing me a dollar bill. I hand him his change and a copy of the paper, which he glances at while I ask, "Do you have any news for us this week?"

He thinks, still scanning the paper. "Pretty quiet here. I heard the Olsons were getting a new puppy. They're the red house over there. Might be something to check out."

"Thanks. And do you have a quote for us?"

One of our regular features is a listing of quotes from people in the neighborhood. Most of them are things like *"We had a great time in California!"* or *"Congratulations to Josie on her graduation!"* The first time I asked Mr. DiFuria for a quote, he recited a line of poetry and we put it in the paper. Dad, who is a stickler for these things, had us run a correction in the next issue. We wrote this up and placed it at the bottom of the second page, next to some clip-art of a guy in jail.

DEPARTMENT OF CORRECTIONS

In the previous issue, we attributed a quote ('Let me not to the marriage of true minds admit impediments.') to Mr. L. DiFuria of 36 Springbrook Dr. The quote is actually from the late Mr. W. Shakespeare of Stratford-on-Avon, England. We apologize for the error.

Mr. DiFuria thinks about it a second. "Life is beautiful if you give it a chance to be."

I have my pod out and am about to turn on the recorder. I ask him, "Is that another famous quote that we're going to have to run a correction on?"

"No! Honest to Betsy, I just made it up. If you find that in Shakespeare anywhere, he stole it from me."

I turn on the recorder and speak. "This is Mr. DiFuria with a quote."

"Let me see if I can do this again," he says. "Life is beautiful if you give it the chance to be."

I thank him, turn off the recorder and wish him a good day. As I leave his porch, I consider asking him to say Hi to Mrs. DiFuria for me, but decide against it.

Dad is the original newspaper person in the family. He was a reporter and news writer before I was born. Now his job is to play the banjo. I think he was surprised to learn he could make more money playing the banjo than writing for the newspaper. He says, "Sometimes you just never know." I'm going to attribute that to Dad, knowing that there's a risk I may need to be corrected.

Dad knows about newspapers and he consults with us a lot. He also bought the heavy-duty printer we use and gets top billing on our masthead, which is as follows:

THE THOMSON ACRES TRIBUNE

Mr. K. McAlpine   *Publisher*

Brian McAlpine   *Editor*

Darren McAlpine	*Deputy Editor*
Beth McAlpine	*Princess*

Mr. K. McAlpine is my Dad. Brian is my older brother. Beth is our little sister. She didn't have much say about her title when we started the paper, but she seems pretty happy about it now. I'm not sure she will be forever. My Mom does not appear on the masthead.

I'm Darren. I like the title Deputy Editor. It sounds like a cross between a newspaper man and a hero in a Western.

Dad told us we should each write our own resume and obituary. Here is my current obit:

DARREN MCALPINE

Darren McAlpine (11) of 24 Glenbrook Road has died. Darren was a sixth grader at Putnam Hills School and Deputy Editor of the Thomson Acres Tribune. Over the past year, he has participated successfully in town soccer and baseball teams and in the Putnam Hills Science Challenge Team. He was also an acolyte at St. Mary's Episcopal Church. Cause of death has not yet been determined, but speculation is centering on complications associated with long-term broccoli poisoning. Throughout his life, his loving but misguided parents insisted that he eat staggering quantities of the vegetable, despite his clear and consistent statements that it was killing him. Darren is survived by his parents, Karl and Patrice McAlpine, and his siblings, Brian and Elizabeth McAlpine, and the family dog, Johann Sebastian Bark.

The next house is 34 Springbrook, the Carlsens. I mostly stick to one side of a street at a time, even though it will mean doubling back later.

The Carlsen house is superficially similar to the DiFuria house. Most of the houses in Thomson Acres were built around the same time by the same builder. But the feel of the house is very different. Everything you see at the DiFuria house looks just so, and the place feels timeless and removed, like a library. The

Carlsen house is pretty much the opposite. As I approach the house, I see a kitchen chair in the front yard on a piece of bare dirt next to the lamppost with their house number. It looks like somebody used the chair to replace the bulb in the lamppost and forgot to put the chair back in the house. This could happen to anyone, but the chair has been there for a couple of weeks now.

I knock on the door and hope to get Mr. Carlsen. He calls me Doogie Howser which I don't like, but he's nice enough and usually buys a paper. Every so often he'll be gone and Mrs. Carlsen will answer the door. I think she works on a funny schedule, so when she answers the door she's usually in a robe looking mad that I've woken her up, which makes me feel like a bad person. Who am I to go around waking up hard-working people so that they can pay me money for a few pages of neighborhood almost-news? Also, she makes me explain about the paper each time like she's never heard of it before, and then she usually doesn't buy one or offer any news.

I knock again, a little louder this time. Immediately, I hear somebody shouting and Mrs. Carlsen appears, wearing a bathrobe and with something bizarre on her head. It looks like she's wearing a shower cap with holes in it. Portions of her hair have been pulled through the holes and rolled around large rollers which have then been encased in clear plastic sandwich bags. She reminds me of the picture of Medusa the Gorgon that appears on the cover of the Greek mythology book we've been studying this semester in Language Arts class.

"Oh, hello," she says. "What is it?"

"I'm with the Thomson Acres Tribune," I say. "The new edition is just out today. Fifty cents a copy. I'm also a reporter and would be interested if you have any news for our next edition."

She gives me a serious and very direct stare. Maybe the baggies are blunting her full effect. I don't turn to stone.

"You're a reporter?" she asks.

"Yes."

This seems to stump her. Meanwhile, I'm thinking, *'Just let me go. I've got lots more houses to get to.'*

"Who are you a reporter for?" she asks.

"I'm a reporter for the Thomson Acres Tribune. All the news of the neighborhood."

She looks at me like I'm speaking gibberish. "That's some kind of a newspaper?" She asks.

"Yes. It's a neighborhood newspaper."

She scrunches up her face. "This neighborhood?"

"Yes. It's the neighborhood newspaper for this street and all of Thomson Acres. Would you like to see a copy?" I pull a copy out of my bag. I don't normally like to let people see the paper unless they've paid first, but I'm worried about getting trapped on the Carlsen porch for the rest of my life.

She stares at the paper I've handed her. The front page headline is 'Meet the Clarks' – with the subhead 'Family from Ohio Moves Into Former Johnston House'.

At this point, even though I'm eager to get going, I'm also curious to see how Mrs. Carlsen will react to the paper. This is now a market test. Maybe she'll look at the attractively laid out and saddle-stitched document in her hand and think it looks surprisingly professional. Maybe she'll look at that headline and think to herself, 'I should buy this. I should know what's going on in my own neighborhood.' On the other hand, maybe the subhead will make her feel bad because she didn't know the Johnstons and doesn't have a clue which house they used to live in.

She looks up from the paper and eyes me suspiciously. "Does this have anything to do with cats?"

One of the reasons I wanted to be a newspaper reporter in the first place is that I would rather be the one asking the questions. People start asking you questions and sometimes there's no good answer. I had a True/False test last year and one of the questions was 'Do birds eat lunch?' There's no good answer to that question, even if you aren't limited to Yes or No.

"Not exactly," I say. "Sometimes we might have a story about a cat."

Mrs. Carlsen sighs and looks up at the sky directly over my head. "They had something on the radio about a scam. People call you and pretend they're from the vet's. They say your little Tinkerbell is going to die unless you get her some medicine that has to be ordered special. Of course, you're in a panic at this point and give your credit card number."

"It's just a newspaper," I say. "It's nothing about your cat."

"We don't have a cat," says Mrs. Carlsen, looking down on me with her eyebrows arching up. What I hear in her voice is: *'Some neighborhood reporter you are.'*

In my defense, I believe that the Carlsens go through pets the way other families go through cartons of orange juice. I believe they have a serial zoo buried in their backyard. I believe that if Noah had married Mrs. Carlsen there would be no animals in the world today.

This is the point where I should remind her that the paper is fifty cents and ask again if she has any news. Only I don't like to repeat myself. It seems disrespectful to me – like I don't think the person can remember what I said one minute ago. So instead I stand there trying to think of something else I could say.

"Do have a quote for us? Or you can also buy an ad if you want." That's the remaining sort of business we could transact. I sell papers, get news and sell ads. Not a lot of people buy ads, but some people do. Mostly it's people who want to advertise some kind of small business. Sometimes a family will run an ad to say Congratulations to a graduate or Happy Anniversary or something like that.

"An ad?" She's looking at me again like I'm speaking a foreign language.

"You don't have to. I just wanted to give you all your options." I drum my fingers on the shoulder strap of my paper bag. "So, you want to buy the paper or can I take it back?"

She hands me the paper. "There is no Tinkerbell," she says. "I just made that part up."

As I head back to the street, I'm thinking about Mom. She has more in common with Mrs. Carlsen than I really like to think about. Take your favorite, funny female television star and get her to play Mrs. Carlsen in the movie of the week and you have my Mom.

"I have a question for you," she said to me the night before.

"O.K."

"The Deevers are having a party. You know the Deevers – Pat and Mitchell. Mitchell knew your Dad in college. Pat's some kind of a pet psychologist, which I've been assured is a real thing. None of us can figure out what Mitchell does. Maybe he's a spy or maybe he comes from enough money that he doesn't have to do anything. Anyway, they have a theme party every year. Everybody dresses up as something from the theme and people try to guess what you are. Actually, you know, Mitchell does something with office buildings. Commercial real estate. But not like Bud Long, who does those horrible strip malls. I suppose they make a lot of money, but ugly, ugly. Also, they have the nicest pair of cavalier spaniels. Those Deevers. Last year, the theme was Nations of the World. Some people who don't quite get it dress up like they're from Italy or wherever, but the real idea is that you're supposed to dress up like the name of a country. So you slick your hair back and you're Greece or you put on some tail feathers and a wattle and you're Turkey. Last year, I was in rags and carrying a print of a Marc Chagall painting."

She cocked her head and looked at me, giving me a chance to figure it out.

"No idea."

"Poor-Chagall. Poor-Chagall. Portugal. I personally thought it was much better than your Dad, who wore a tee shirt and was Chile. Although, of course, that had a certain simple elegance about it. People were baffled by mine. Mostly they seemed to think I was trying to make a point about starving artists. I thought the best one was Claire Mogor. She had a tray with a glass of water and a bowl of ice and an electric tea kettle and a big, domed lid. She got some steam going from the kettle and then covered it all with the lid and it was The United States."

"That's good," I said. "I like that."

"Chloe Deever babysat for you kids when Beth was a baby. Cute as a button, but I think she's married now."

"That's OK," I said.

"Anyway, this year the theme is Movie Stars and that [darn], simple-elegant father of yours is drawing circles on the side of his face and going as Cheek O Marks. Personally, I would have put o-marks on a grouch or a harp, which would have been slightly less obscure, but it was his idea, and he's putting them on his cheek. So here's my question."

"My point, and I do have one..." I said.

"Have you ever heard of Tallulah Bankhead?"

"No. Great name, though."

"So maybe she's too obscure?"

I shrugged. "Maybe."

"OK, Question Two. Was Lucille Ball a movie star?"

"Hold on," I said. "Lucille Ball. She's the *I Love Lucy* lady, right? What's the question?"

"Would she count as a movie star?"

"I don't know. Maybe if you're a big enough TV star it counts as being a movie star. Why? What would your costume be?"

"I don't know. Something with a seal and a ball in a bathroom in England."

So now I'm at 32 Springbrook. The place used to be perfect like the DiFuria's, but now it's slipping a little. Mrs. Everett lives there. I ring the bell and wait. Mrs. Everett isn't a fast person. Eventually, the door swings back and her head peaks around. She's short and wears her white hair back in a bun. She'd be a perfect illustration of a little old lady except she's always wearing a tracksuit.

"Good morning," she says. "It's so nice to see you again!"

I love coming here. She makes me feel like I'm the highlight of her week. I suppose that could be depressing, but it's not depressing to me. I like being the highlight of somebody's week.

"Hi, Mrs. Everett," I say. "I've got the new Thomson Acres Tribune. Would you like a paper today?"

"I would love one of your papers! I wish the regular paper was half as good as the paper you boys make for us. I don't know how we got so lucky to have you boys making this wonderful paper for us in this neighborhood. Let me go get my wallet. Wait here."

And then she stops, pauses for a moment, and then turns back to me. "Or you could come in. Would you like some soup?"

I would love to sit down and have some soup with Mrs. Everett, but I can't. I'm on duty. "I'm sorry. I need to keep doing my route. Thanks for the offer, though."

"Let me go get my wallet. I'll be back in just a sec."

Thomson Acres is built along the side of a big hill, pretty close to the Skumish Reservoir. If you ask people why they live in Thomson Acres, one of the answers you'll hear a lot is that it's close to the reservoir and state forest, which has swimming in the summer and hiking in the woods all year. When I think of the reservoir, I think of it like a time bomb or like a big sword over our heads. When I was in third grade, my class took a field trip to the reservoir offices and they had a big model of the reservoir and surrounding area and all you had to do was look at the model and you could see that we were doomed. One good earthquake, one carefully placed terrorist bomb, one miscalculation of how high the water can safely be allowed to get, and Whoosh! No more Thomson Acres. We might as well be living on the side of an active volcano.

Just to rub it in, the house behind us and further up the hill, the Schipkes on Thomson Road, has a swimming pool. I can look up from my back yard and see the retaining wall that keeps their pool from washing away our back yard.

I hope the reservoir holds until I grow up and move away. I know that sounds horrible, like I don't care what happens to anyone else. When I'm working on the paper, I think of it sometimes as a way to preserve the everyday history of a place that people may wonder about someday. The Pompeii Times.

For some reason, when I think about Thomson Acres washing away, I get saddest thinking about Mrs. Everett. This doesn't make any sense, because she's had a nice long life. I should feel sadder about the kids in the neighborhood. I should feel saddest about my own family. Maybe it's because I assume that the kids and my family members will get away somehow. Even in her tracksuit, it's hard to imagine Mrs. Everett outrunning a flood.

She's back at the door, holding out a dollar bill to me. I take the bill and hand her a paper and start reaching in my pocket for change.

"Oh, keep the change!" she says with a wave. "I just love your paper. Keep the change and it's still a bargain!"

I thank her and move on, feeling even sorrier for poor Mrs. Everett, washed away to smithereens.

I get a kick out of doing the newspaper, but it's not a particularly cool thing to do. At my school, the terms "cool" and "popular" are used pretty much interchangeably, but I don't think they should be. The cool kids are powerful but not necessarily popular in the sense of being liked by a lot of people.

Brian's theory is that life is a biathlon. That's an event where you cross-country ski and then shoot a rifle. Cross-country skiing is all about putting yourself out there. People with King Kong large-motor aggressiveness are going to be way ahead mid-way through a biathlon. But then comes the shooting, which is all about deliberation and focus.

His theory is that everything up through high school graduation is the skiing competition and everything after that is the shooting competition. It's a pretty cool theory. I believe he came up with it while watching *Revenge of the Nerds* during the Winter Olympics.

The next house, 30 Springbrook, is the Bumgarners. They have a carport next to their garage that's completely filled with a houseboat that Mr. Bumgarner has been building since as long as I can remember. I think of Mr. Bumgarner like Noah, building this big, crazy boat on his own. I'm not sure how it would ever get moved out of the carport. It's like a really big version of a ship in a bottle. Mr. Bumgarner may be thinking like me about the reservoir and figures that in case of emergency he and his family could use the boat like an escape pod.

Trish Bumgarner answers the door. I think she's a freshman in high school this year. She has a brother who's away at college. There's some music on in the room behind her that sounds like her music and not her parents' music. I don't particularly know or like Trish Bumgarner and she doesn't seem that pretty to me, but she's still a girl in high school. I stand up straight and try to get a little depth to my voice.

"Hi," I say. "Want a paper?"

She shrugs. "Sure."

I reach for a copy. "It's fifty cents."

She looks disappointed, like I tricked her. Brian has a line he likes to use when people complain about the paper costing fifty cents. He says: "I'll make you a special deal – two for a dollar." He has a way of saying a line like that that makes people feel like they're in on the joke. I tried saying it once and it didn't work at all. I just sounded like a jerk.

"I thought we had a subscription," she says.

I shrug. "You're probably thinking of the Courant. Or maybe the New York Times."

"Oh. Just a second."

She disappears, leaving the door open. I guess they don't have a dog. Then she sticks her head back out. "Come in and meet my friends," she says, and then disappears again.

This does not make any sense to me, but I don't feel like I have a lot of choice. I ease slowly into the house. The entryway connects to a hallway and a living room and everything is happening in the living room. Music is playing and the TV is on and the room is full of girls who are older than I am. They all seem to be wearing bathrobes and talking at the same time.

I gape for a while and try to follow voices.

"So mean – it was ridiculous!"

"N.K. That's Not Kidding."

"Like a big, fat goose! A goose! You know, with the crazy beak that like goes up to its forehead."

"Who's that?"

"I don't know. Is that someone's brother? Are you someone's brother?"

"Who's that?"

"Is that like a neighbor kid? Are you a neighbor kid?"

"Can he talk? Hey, kid! Can you talk?"

I get good grades and I write a lot of the Tribune and I like to think of myself as a pretty smart person, a person who can put words together in an orderly way as needed. However, there's this thing that happens to me sometimes. If too much is happening around me, my brain pretty much shuts down.

"Hey Trish! Your boyfriend is here!"

"Can he talk? Is this kid retarded?"

"Hey! Don't make fun of retarded kids! They can't help it."

"I like his purse! It's like a man-bag, only it's a boy-bag."

"Whacha got in your bag?"

"Whacha got in your boy-bag?"

I hold up a copy of the paper.

"What is that?"

"It's a little newspaper!"

"Thomson Acres Tribune. You're [kidding] me! Thomson Acres has a newspaper?"

She actually says something stronger than "kidding". As a journalist, I want to be accurate, but as deputy editor of a neighborhood newspaper I keep everything printable.

"That's right. Thomson Acres has a neighborhood newspaper," says Trish, who has returned from some other part of the house and is holding two quarters pinched between her thumb and index finger. "This is somebody-or-other McAlpine..."

She looks at me and raises her eyebrows. "Darren," I say.

"This is Darren McAlpine. He has a special deal for us today. For fifty cents, you can get a copy of the Thomson Acres newspaper and also a big, wet kiss on the lips from Darren McAlpine!"

There's much squealing at this. This would be a good time to find out that I have a superpower, like the ability to de-materialize.

"And if we buy five or more papers from him, Darren McAlpine has agreed to do Bloody Mary!"

The squealing gets louder and then turns into a chant.

"Bloody Mary! Bloody Mary! Bloody Mary!"

Where are Trish's parents? Roomfuls of girls shouldn't be left unsupervised. Bad things could happen.

"I'm in!"

"Who has fifty cents?"

"He's a twerp! This is child molesting!"

"It's just a kiss. Don't get carried away!"

"I don't care if he's a twerp. It's worth it just for Bloody Mary!"

"Hold on, hold on, hold on!" says Trish. She ducks out of the room and then returns a moment later with a metal can that she shakes like a maraca. "This is the family change can. You can take fifty cents out if you want, but you have to pay me back." She looks across the room and stares at someone. "Janelle?" Trish raises her eyebrows and makes a shaking noise with the can.

The girl who must be Janelle stands up and pulls on the belt of her robe. The other girls are making noises while Janelle makes a funny face. "You know," says Janelle, "I could really use a newspaper!" The other girls hoot and cheer while she walks over to Trish, fishes two quarters out of the can, says "I'll pay you back on Monday" to Trish, and walks over to me. "Here's fifty cents," she says and hands me the two quarters. I pocket them and hand her a paper. "Thanks," she says and then leans down and covers my mouth with her mouth and does something to my hair. After a moment, she leans back, gives me a look and turns away. "Keep

16

the change!" she says and walks back to where she was sitting while all the girls clap and hoot.

My face is wet, but I'm thinking it would be lame to wipe my mouth on my sleeve. Also, I'm struggling to understand what she meant by 'Keep the change.' The paper is fifty cents or – according to Trish – the paper and big, wet kiss from me is fifty cents. Either way, it's fifty cents. But the girls all laughed like "Keep the change," has another, probably dirty, meaning.

One of the things that happens to you as an eleven-year-old is that you're present when rude jokes are told that you don't get. I believe this may happen more than usual if you have an older brother and also a father who performs in places where people drink alcohol. Last night, Dad was telling a joke where the punch line was a girl saying to her boyfriend something like, *'All right, you can come with us if you want to, but we're all going to get Brazilians!'*

You need to walk a fine line when this happens. It is phony and potentially dangerous to laugh at a joke you don't understand. On the other hand, you don't want to be a buzz-kill sourpuss. So I try to mold my face into a wise and knowing smile. It could be the smile of someone who gets the joke but has heard it before or it could be the smile of someone who just likes to see other people laughing and having a good time.

I assume that a Brazilian can be something different than just a person from Brazil. As an experiment, this morning I tried asking my little sister, Beth, what a Brazilian is. She thought for a moment and then told me that it's a really, really big number.

Trish looks around the room, then zeroes in on somebody and shakes the can. "Megan?"

The girl who must be Megan rises silently. She walks slowly to Trish, takes some money from the can and leans in towards Trish. "You are a bad influence on us all," she says. She walks over to me and hands me the coins. I pocket the coins and hand her a paper. She takes the paper with one hand and with her other hand she takes my hand – the one that had just handed her the paper – and puts it behind her neck as she leans in and puts her mouth over my mouth.

"Bad influence!" yells one of the girls as Megan slides her mouth around on my face. Then Megan straightens up and I let my hand drop from her neck.

I'm wondering if Trish is the bad influence or if somehow I'm the bad influence. My face is pretty wet. Trish is looking around again. The girls point and shout names for who should go next. Mostly they are pointing at and shouting the name of Monica. Trish is rattling the can again, but there's a stir from another direction.

"They're back!"

A door opens in another room and I hear people moving. Then Mr. and Mrs. Bumgarner are standing in the living room. They have bags of what looks like groceries and are looking around trying to figure out what is going on. I'm not sure if Trish is in trouble or if I'm in trouble. Mrs. Bumgarner is half as tall as Mr. Bumgarner, but she's the scary one. Being short, she looks me straight in the eyes.

"And who are you?" She is looking dead at me, but somehow I can tell that she is speaking to her daughter.

"He's-"

"I asked him," says Mrs. Bumgarner, without looking away from me.

"I'm Darren McAlpine." I wait a moment. No response. "I live on Glenbrook Road," I say.

"Where's your Mom?" she asks.

I'm not sure it's Mrs. Bumgarner's business where my Mom is. "She's around." Another pause. "I'm here with the new issue of the Thomson Acres Tribune." I pull one out of my bag and hold it up as proof.

Mrs. Bumgarner looks around, then looks back at me. "And did we buy a copy?"

I have to think about this one. "Not yet," I say. "A couple of your guests bought copies."

"Oh really," she says. She looks around and two girls hold up their copies.

"Well, let's go out to the front step," she says, and I follow her around the corner and out the front door. "How much?"

"Fifty cents."

She hands me a dollar. I have plenty of coins in my pocket to give her the right change. I don't ask about news or quotes or ads. I say, "Thank you," and head on to the Fandells at 28 Springbrook.

My face feels weird and I'm a little out of breath, but the first thing that's in my mind from my time at the Bumgarner house is the phrase "your guests." I feel really good about that. Not "these girls" or "Trish's friends." There was some kind of ju-jitsu power in identifying the paper buyers to Mrs. Bumgarner as "your guests." I like it when I can get words right under pressure. I say it again to myself: "A couple of your guests bought copies." No need to change a word.

There's a lady at my church who is so good at arranging flowers that even I notice. It's like a magic trick. Take a big vase and a bunch of flowers and turn them into something that looks like a picture in a museum. That's what I want to be. I want to be the church flower lady of words on a deadline.

Nobody answers the door at the Fandells. We have an arrangement with them, so I leave a paper on their doormat and head to number 26, Mrs. Luebker.

When the Fandells came back from their vacation to Florida, I asked Mr. Fandell about their trip and he said, "It was great! We went to St. Augustine and saw the state capitol!"

Quotes don't need to be fact-checked the same way you'd fact-check a statement in a news story. I'm guessing that Mr. Fandell said capitol with an "o" meaning the building and not capital with an "a" meaning the city. Copy editing from a young age has been teaching me so many of these fine distinctions that I expect to be the most boring person in the world by the time I get to be a grown-up. Either way – capital or capitol – it didn't sound right in a statement about St. Augustine. State capitals is one of the topics where kids tend to do better than grown-ups. In fact, I think I'm starting to get a little rusty on them already. I knew them all cold when I was a third grader.

If those were my own words, I'd just correct St. Augustine to Tallahassee. But if I change the name of the city, then I'm misquoting Mr. Fandell. Also, a little Googling tells me that St. Augustine was sort-of the state capital before Tallahassee, so it's possible that Mr. Fandell was referring to a former capitol building that really is in St. Augustine.

In this case, my answer was to run the quote but help it along as gently as possible:

> The Fandells had a good trip to Florida. "It was great!" said Mr. Fandell. "We went to St. Augustine. And we saw the state capitol!"

As I'm walking to 26 Springbrook, I'm thinking about all those girls at the Bumgarners. Even though it was uncomfortable and embarrassing, I didn't mind the kissing business. I wanted them all to kiss me. I mean, why not? It's better than being kissed by one of my aunts. What's bothering me is the money. I'm pretty sure it's wrong to get kissed for money. I'm guessing it would be worse if I were a girl. I'm not sure if selling kisses is, in fact, actually a worse thing for girls to do, or if it just seems worse the way most bad things seem worse if a girl does them.

As I get closer to 26, I look back and see Mr. Fandell gardening in his side yard. Should I double back or not? I already dropped off a paper there. Then he looks up in my direction, so I head over to him.

"Hey!" I say when I'm close enough. "I didn't see you over here. I dropped the paper off."

"Thanks," he says.

"You got any news for us?" I ask.

He looks at the bush he's trimming and doesn't say anything. I wonder if he heard the question. Then he sets down his shears and looks at me. "I don't know if this is your kind of story, but there's something in the neighborhood that I'm worried about."

What does he mean it might not be our kind of story? Maybe he thinks we can't handle anything tougher than a cat up a tree. "What is it?" I ask.

"Jeff got invited to a meeting tonight at Kyle Butler's house." Jeff is one of the Fandell boys. He's in high school – I don't know what year. The Butlers live on Glenview, which is in Thomson Acres but over on Brian's route. Kyle is also in high school and is known for organizing protests. "He says the meeting is about deer hunting. Kyle and some of the others are against the hunting and they want to find a way to interfere with it somehow. I don't know what they're thinking about, but I'm just worried that protesting kids and hunters out to shoot a deer – that could be a dangerous mix, you know?"

"Sure," I say, although I'm distracted by a voice in my head saying "Bloody Mary!" What was that about? Maybe it has something to do with their periods.

"So, if it's a meeting, maybe the paper ought to cover it. Just a thought. It's seven-thirty at the Butlers," says Mr. Fandell.

"Thanks," I say and head off. I think about saying something like 'Have a nice day' but I want him to think that we're serious enough to handle stuff like guns and kids in danger.

For the rest of my route, when I'm not actually looking somebody in the eye I'm thinking about Bumgarner stuff – Bloody Mary, Keep the Change – but also how I'm going to get permission to go out and cover Kyle Butler's meeting. It's a tricky one. If I were my kid, I don't know that I'd let me go out on a Saturday night without an invitation to a house full of high school kids.

When I get home, I hear Mom in the kitchen. I call out, "I'm home!"

"Good," she says. "Want some lunch? I just got the peanut butter stirred up. It was a good workout. I'm ready to arm wrestle an alligator!"

"Sure," I say. Then, "I don't think alligators have arms." Then, "Can I go over to the Butler's house tonight? Kyle Butler is having a meeting about protesting deer hunting and Mr. Fandell thinks it might make a good story for the Tribune."

That was the best I could come up with. I figured it might help to insert Mr. Fandell's name.

"How's your homework?" she asks.

"Good. I'm caught up in everything."

"Do the Butlers know you're coming?"

"No."

"Strawberry or raspberry?"

"Honey and banana," I say.

"One super-duper coming up!" Then, "You can't just show up at the Butlers if they aren't expecting you. I'll call Janie."

Mom knows everybody in the neighborhood. She should be writing the newspaper. Somehow, she is making the sandwich and dialing the phone.

"Hello, is Janie there? This is Pat McAlpine. Thank you so much." Slice banana, slice banana, slice banana. "Janie! Pat McAlpine. Is this a good time? I just have a very quick question for you. Do alligators have arms? Actually, that's not the question. It's just something Darren and I were having a joke about. Anyway, you know the neighborhood paper that our boys put out? The newspaper. That's right. Anyway, our Darren has heard about a meeting that he thinks will be at your house tonight and he wants to cover it for the newspaper. I mean, maybe they'll write about it and maybe they won't. They never quite know and don't like to promise anything. Does that make any sense? Sure. So I just wanted to check this out with you first." Squeeze the honey. Spread the honey. Top slice. Cut into two more-or-less triangles. "Uh-huh. Uh-huh." Sandwich on plate. Napkin folded in half. "Great! That's very kind of you. Seven-thirty? Right. Well, I don't want to use up your whole day, I just wanted to check about that. What? That's right – front legs, arms – what's the difference, really? Forelimbs, maybe. They're sort of like arms, aren't they? Yes, and to you as well! Yes, thank you. Thank you."

She hangs up and sets the sandwich in front of me. I'm in awe. I feel bad about comparing Mom to Mrs. Carlsen just because she throws in some non-sequiturs. A good plumber uses every tool in the box.

"Janie says that Kyle always likes press coverage for his causes, so you're welcome to go over there."

"Tha!" I say through a bite of sandwich.

After lunch, I look to see if Brian is in his room. He's two years older than me but three years ahead of me in school. I stand a respectful distance outside the door and listen. I can hear the faint sound of non-amplified electric guitar riffs. Brian is a musician. He may be a rock star someday, if rock star is still a thing when he grows up.

He has a poster of Jimi Hendrix. Don't feel bad if you have to look him up. He also has an old movie poster of Robert Redford and Dustin Hoffman as Woodward and Bernstein. I love that poster because Woodward and Bernstein were a famous newspaper team, so I figure that must be Brian and me. I'm not sure which one I am. The short, skinny one, I guess.

Mom is pretty smart, but my aunt, her sister, was such a genius from such a young age that she was a local celebrity. People would ask Mom whether or not she was the smart one, which she says didn't bother her. She'd reply, "No, I'm the cute one!" I think about my year-ahead, musical prodigy brother sometimes and wonder if I need to figure out how to be the cute one.

"Dalrymple!" he calls. That's his nickname for me.

"Yes," I say.

"Name that tune!" He starts playing something on his guitar. I enter his room to hear it better. An electric guitar without an amp is whisper quiet.

"You know I suck at this game," I say.

"Get two out of five and - Bam! – we call you a winner. Here – we'll start with this."

He changes over to an elaborate riff with a lot of stretched notes. It could be *Mary Had a Little Lamb* and I wouldn't recognize it played that way.

I shrug. "I got nothing."

"Ooch! You do suck at this game," he says. "That's my approximation of the Hendrix version of *The Star Spangled Banner.*"

I stare at him blankly.

"*O, say can you see by the dawn's early light?* It's our national anthem."

"Yeah," I say. "I should have known it."

"Lucky for you that you were born a citizen. You'd never pass the test. I need to make this easier." He plucks out a simple version of Happy Birthday.

"*Stairway to Heaven!*" I say. "Look, I want to touch base on a couple of things from my Tribune rounds this morning."

He says OK and pulls the strap over his head and sets the guitar on its stand.

"When I got to the Bumgarners, Trish was having some kind of sleep-over and her folks were off shopping or something. It was kind of a crazy scene."

"Mmmm. Sounds interesting. Who was there?"

"I don't know most of their names. There was a Janelle."

"Coops. Janelle Cooper," he says. "She thinks she's very hot stuff."

"And a Monica."

He rubs his nose. "Could be a couple of Monicas. Was she half-Korean?"

I shrug. "I don't know."

"Good!" he says, which surprises me because usually he wants me to know everything. "I'm thinking that's a pretty boy-crazy group. Did they attack you?"

I'm torn. I want to tell him and I don't want to tell him.

"Two of them kissed me," I say.

"Woo-kachee! Congratulations!" he says, shaking my hand like I just won an award. "That could be our next lead story."

"Trish's parents came home or it would have been more."

"The Bumgarners," says Brian. "An interesting family. That boat is, like, Mr. Bumgarner's man-cave. He goes in there and watches dirty movies or something. Maybe he just needs to get away. Mrs. Bumgarner seems like she's pretty intense."

"Anyway, I didn't want you to hear something about it at school and not hear it from me first."

He points at me. "Interesting question. Will I hear anything about this at school? Yes-no? Yes-no? On the one hand – not a story that any of those girls want to tell. No offense, but you're a sixth grader. On the other hand – news wants to be told. This is the basis of all journalism." He stops and gives me a look. "You're OK, though, right? They didn't attack you, attack you?"

"No, I'm OK," I say.

I'm not sure exactly what he is thinking about, but I have stuff that I wonder about. Someday I want to get married and be all sexy with my wife and eventually have kids and all that. You see a lot of grown-up men on TV commercials saying that they have problems being sexy with their wives. The good thing is that they have pills for it. I'm OK with needing a pill if it comes to that. I have friends who have to take a pill before they can take a history test.

"There's something else, unrelated," I say.

"Shoot."

"Kyle Butler is having some kind of anti-deer-hunting meeting tonight. Mr. Fandell put me onto it because Jeff Fandell is planning to go. I talked to Mom about it and she called Mrs.

Butler and got permission for me to go over and cover the meeting for the paper. Is that OK with you?"

"Go for it! Kangaroo entrails!" he says. "I couldn't go tonight, anyway. I expect to hear that at least two of those deer-loving high school girls kiss you tonight!"

'Kangaroo entrails' means 'I like it'. At one point over the summer, Brian said to me: "We need a code. Some kind of secret language. Only it shouldn't look like a code. See what you can figure out."

Dad and Brian both like to give me puzzles and challenges, and mostly I like to get them. I thought about the code for a few days and came back to him with a piece of paper.

"This is our code," I said and handed him the paper. On the paper was written:

> *Tim has incredibly silly ideas: silent orchestras, underwater robot cars, operas during eclipses.*

"This is our code?" he asked.

I gave him a look and ran my finger under the words on the paper. "This is our code."

The next day he left a piece of paper on the desk in my room:

> *Ivan lives inside kangaroo entrails in Turkey!*

I'm standing on the sidewalk, two houses away from the Butlers and reach into my sport coat pocket and pull out my pod to check the time. It's 7:24. Still too early to walk over to their door, although I've seen a few cars pull up already and some big kids go into the house. They're dressed funny and act a little crazy.

As a kid, each year you get smarter and better at things. I used to think that was the pattern and that it would go on forever. Now I see that the world runs in cycles. The moon gets bigger and then it gets smaller. Days get longer and then they get shorter. We get smarter and then we get to be teenagers. We start getting stupider and worse at things. We stop being friendly and we deliberately make ourselves less attractive looking. This worries me a lot. What can I do? I worry about this the way Dad worries about ending up like his aunt who has Alzheimer's. I'm not sure there's a lot that either one of us can do. I guess we should just enjoy thinking straight for as long as we can.

Most kids either don't notice or don't care. They can't wait to get older. This makes no sense to me. It's like being impatient in the dentist's waiting room. What's the hurry?

I ring the bell at 7:30. The door is opened by a high school kid with tattoos of Asian writing on his arms. I don't think he's a Butler. I think he was there for the meeting and was standing by the door when the bell rang.

"Come in. You – um – here for the meeting?" he asks.

"Yeah."

"Everybody's going down in the basement." He points the way.

On a show I saw recently, they asked a guy about a supermodel with a name that sounds like a terrorist group. If she would be his girlfriend, would he tattoo her universally hated name on his arm? I, personally, would not mind having a girlfriend with an embarrassing name, but it's crazy for anybody to tattoo a girlfriend's name on their arm. Tattoos in general are crazy. They are way too permanent. I don't like to write in ink. If I had a car, I wouldn't put any bumper stickers on it. They're too hard to take off. You think something is smart or funny today, but it might not seem so great in a year or two.

The Butler main floor looks like the living room section of a furniture store, but downstairs is another story. There's a big, open area with a folded-up ping pong table shoved against the wall. There are some area rugs over a concrete floor. There are a bunch of different kinds of chairs – folding chairs, kitchen table chairs, bean bag chairs – arranged in a semi-circle. Two guys are horsing around hitting a ping pong ball back and forth in the air and another half dozen teenage boys and girls are sitting in the chairs, playing with their phones. I sit on a folding chair and pull out my pod. "Let me see if I can do this again," says Mr. DiFuria in my ear. "Life is beautiful if you give it the chance to be."

I see Kyle come down the stairs, talk to someone and then go back up again. Later on, Tattoo Arm Guy comes down twice to check on things. Finally, Kyle and Tattoo Arm Guy come down together. Kyle is holding some papers in his hand. He walks to the point where the chairs are pointing. It's about ten of eight.

"Thanks for coming out tonight," says Kyle. "I was hoping for some more, but I think we should get started."

And then Kyle talks. If you watched a video of his talk with the sound turned down, you'd think he was a terrible speaker. He doesn't look at anybody. He's looking at his papers and then looking up at the ceiling. His hair is short on the sides but very long on top and it keeps falling in his face and then every so often he shoves it back and it's out of the way for five seconds and then back in his face again.

But if you listened to a voice recording, you'd probably think it was a pretty good talk. He organizes his thoughts and picks his words carefully and makes his case point by point.

Deer, he tells us, are intelligent and beautiful creatures that have been in this area longer than people. Meanwhile, hunting subjects deer to cruel pain and unnatural disruptions to their family life. Hunting is dangerous and bad for the environment. He says it's also a bad way to control the deer population. He says that the government bureaus that oversee hunting are funded by hunting licenses and that actually creates an incentive for the state to encourage overpopulation of deer.

I don't know if he's making sense or not. I wish this was one of those news shows where they have another guy who takes the opposite position. All I can come up with in my head is a guy who stands up and says, "Deer are ugly, vicious creatures who love getting shot!"

Finally, he tells the group what they can do about it. Number One: We should all put our names on his sign-up sheet. No commitment and he'll keep us informed of future events. Number Two: On November 4, which is two weeks from today and one week before opening day of hunting season, he invites everyone to march from the Thomson Acres sign to the parking lot of the state forest. Number Three: He and Brad (who I think is Tattoo Arms

Guy) have decided that they are going to be Deerwalkers. This means that they will wear brown and run around in the woods during hunting season – in the hope that their presence will make hunters afraid to shoot at things they see moving around in the woods. He doesn't say that anyone else should do this, but he doesn't say they shouldn't.

This is when I understand what Mr. Fandell was worried about. Young people posing as deer during hunting season. That's pretty much asking to get shot.

Kyle asks if there are any questions. Everybody looks around. I'm afraid that people might laugh, but I raise my hand.

Kyle points at me. "Yeah?"

I take a breath while I try to edit down the question in my head. "What if you get shot?"

The group laughs quietly, like it's a cute question, which is what I wanted to avoid. Kyle says, "Yes. I'm going to hate that if it happens. I really, really don't want to get shot. But I also want to change this situation, and I'm willing to take the risk. Even if I get shot, my chances are a lot better than the deer we're trying to protect. For one thing, I'm bound to get a lot better medical treatment than a deer would." He looks around. "Any other questions? If not, have a good night everyone."

Nobody claps. People get up and start milling around. I don't see any refreshments. Meredith Green walks over to me. She's the older sister of Darren Green, a friend of mine who lives on our street. He's known in my family as Other Darren. One of the things I like about Other Darren is that he doesn't put on a show or pretend to be anything he isn't. If he gets a bad grade or gets in trouble with his Mom, he just puts it out there. "Man, I got a bad grade," or "Man, I'm in big trouble with my Mom!" It's nice to feel like you have a friend who is a real person.

"Darren McAlpine," she says. She's smiling, but she looks a little nervous. Why is she nervous? Maybe because she talks pretty openly when I see her at the Greens. Who she likes, stuff like that. Maybe she thinks I'm going to out her. "What are you doing here?"

"I'm working," I say. "We might write a story about this for the Tribune. What about you?"

"I'm an animal person. There's plenty of stuff to do in the world without shooting up the woods. Let's just leave the animals alone. I'll tell my brother I saw you." And she's gone.

Who did Meredith say she likes? The thing is, if I think of the name, there's probably a chance I'll accidentally say it out loud. It was an exotic name. Khaleel.

You can't stop yourself from thinking something. Brian will sometimes shout at me, "Don't think about a white gorilla!" Good luck not thinking about a white gorilla. You can, however, stop yourself from saying something out loud. I want to say "Khaleel" out loud but settle for muttering "White Gorilla" to myself.

Some people are leaving. I'd like to interview Kyle's parents. What do they think about their son being a human target? What would Mom say if I told her I was planning to protect the deer by getting hunters to shoot at me? I wouldn't have to worry about the hunters. Before I ever got to the woods, she would kill me.

Upstairs, Mrs. Butler is near the door, schmoozing with people as they leave. "Oh, hello! You're Pat McAlpine's boy."

"Yes," I say. "Hello, Mrs. Butler."

"Are you the musician?"

"No, that's my brother, Brian. I'm Darren."

I think about saying: *I'm the football player.* That would be a joke. I'm short and skinny and weigh about as much as a Welsh Corgi. But Mrs. Butler doesn't really know me and wouldn't know for sure I was making a joke. She might feel like she had to say something encouraging.

"You and your brother do the newspaper together?"

"Yes." I need get a question in here. It's going to seem rude, but I'm about to lose her attention. "Would it be all right to ask you for a quote? What do you think about Kyle's plans?"

"Oh, you know, we are so proud of Kyle and how engaged he is in the community and in the world."

I'm thinking it's too late to pull out my pod or even a notepad. I'm trying to fix her words in my head. Proud. Engaged. Community. World.

"But are you worried about his safety?"

She grabs my upper arm. "I'm his mother!" she says. "I've been worried about his safety since the day he was born."

I hate for people to squeeze my arm because it isn't much of an arm. I like to think the jacket makes me look like I have normal arms, but inside the jacket my arms are like coat hanger wires.

Outside, I say the quotes into my pod as best I can. Once I'm home, I try to write an article:

> *Last Thursday evening, eleven high school students from the area gathered at the Butler's house on Glenview Road to hear Kyle Butler make a presentation about deer hunting. Kyle opposes hunting deer for a variety of reasons, which he explained in some detail. He invited those who share his concerns to participate in a march on Hipkins Road on Saturday, November 4 from the Thomson Acres sign to the state forest parking lot. The march will start at noon.*
>
> *Kyle also said that he and one of his colleagues are planning to be "Deerwalkers." This means that they will walk in brown clothes among the deer in the state forest during hunting season. They hope that their presence will discourage hunters from shooting at the deer.*
>
> *Those wanting more information can contact Kyle at krbutler99@gmail.com.*

I'm not happy with this story. For one thing, it buries the lede. Deerwalking should be in the first sentence. Also, the two "ons" – on Hipkins and on Saturday – are awkward one after the other. Also, I don't like the phrase "among the deer." They could probably run around in the woods all day and not see a deer. Also, the story doesn't use any of the quotes I got.

The main thing I don't like about the story is the lack of a message. If something horrible happens, someone could look back at that story and say that we encouraged it to happen. I picture myself knocking on Mrs. Everett's door. *"Excuse me, ma'am. Would you like to buy a paper with some nice quotes from the kids we lured to their deaths?"*

I don't know how to fix the story, though. Should it be longer? Should it end after the first paragraph? Should it have an accompanying editorial?

Dad has a running bit he does when Brian and I sit down with him to talk about newspaper stuff.

> *Welcome to the Overthinking Department. Well, it's not a department, really. We're more of a hub.*

> *Welcome to the Overthinking Department. Our motto here is – well, we don't actually have a motto. We've been looking at a lot of possible mottoes, but we haven't settled on one yet.*

> *Welcome to the Overthinking Department. My name is – well, actually, what you call me depends on who you are. My wife calls me Punkin. I'm not sure why. I've always taken it as a breezy allusion to my orange pallor and the horny growth on the top of my head.*

Mom calls out that it's time for bed. I turn off the computer and brush my teeth.

2. Not Really a Very Real Paper

Would I rather have my arm cut off or go blind? Declan is a friend at school who is always asking about horrible alternatives like that. When I think about those questions, I want to think them through. In the case of arm vs. blindness, it seems pretty obvious that it would be better to lose an arm. You could live a pretty normal life with one arm. But I'd rather be blind than lose two arms. Where's the tipping point? Is it an arm and a hand? An arm and a couple of fingers? It might make a difference if it's your left arm or your right arm.

Meanwhile, Declan has lost patience with the process. He just wants an answer. Option A or Option B. I'm thinking about Declan Sunday morning, while sitting in my acolyte robe in the front part of the church (church word of the day: *chancel*) listening to a priest in training give a sermon on the difference between Jesus and a suicide bomber. Declan might have put the question as: 'Would you rather die by being nailed to a cross or by being exploded in a crowded marketplace?' I bet there are a lot of churches where people would get upset about hearing 'Jesus' and 'suicide bomber' in the same sentence. Our church is pretty open-minded, especially with earnest priests in training.

Say you're willing to sacrifice your own life to be faithful to a call from God. This sounds very Jesus-like until the preacher mentions the suicide bomber. So what's the difference?

As I listen to the sermon, I'm thinking this might have application for the Deerwalkers. Is Kyle Butler Jesus or is he a suicide bomber? The conclusion seems a little wishy-washy to me. It has to do with love and not hurting other people. Kyle I guess loves the deer and he isn't hurting anyone, so maybe Kyle is Jesus. Still, I don't think Jesus would trick somebody into crucifying him.

Beth shouts that dinner is ready. *"Madame a servi!"* she shouts, as if any of us speaks French. I hightail it to the bathroom. There's family joke that when dinner is called I always need to go to the bathroom. It's not a particularly great joke, but it's pretty much true. What happens is that I get involved in things. So when dinner is announced, it's like being woken up in the morning, and the first thing I need to do at that point is pee.

In the bathroom, I'm thinking that *How to Pee* might be a good name for a book. But you'd still have to write the book, and what would you say?

My parents are determined to have family dinners whenever possible, but always on Sunday. There are times it doesn't seem like it will be a good idea because somebody's fighting with somebody, but the nice thing about dinner is that it's an automatic truce.

Sometimes my family is so weird we're from outer space and sometimes we're so conventional we're from a hundred years ago. Sunday dinner is in the old-fashioned category.

I'm hurrying because everybody will be waiting because we start dinner with Grace. As usual, I'm the last one to the table. Mom and Dad are at opposite ends of an oval table. Brian and Beth are on one side and my place is on the other side.

"We're starving here!" calls out Beth. "He's slow as molasses!"

"Yo! Nice that you could join us this year," says Brian.

"Whose turn?" asks Mom.

"Beth's," says Brian. We take turns saying Grace, and Brian is always the one who remembers whose turn it is. He could be making it up for all I know.

We bow our heads and Beth says the Grace we say. "Blessofatherthesegiftstoouruse andustoyourlovingservice andkeepusevermindfuloftheneedsofothers throughJesusChristOurLordAmen."

We look up and over at Mom. Dinner time is like a late night talk show and Mom is the host. Dad is the celebrity guest. Brian, Beth and I are the sidekicks.

"These are veggie burgers," says Mom. "Very, very healthy for us all. We're all going to be strong as ants. I read somewhere that if an ant were as big as us, it could lift up a railroad car. So that's going to be us – picking up railroad cars left and right. Salad in the bowl. Baked beans in the blue pot. Green beans in the brown pot."

"It should be green beans in the brown pot and brown beans in the green pot," says Dad.

"Ha! Or brown pot in the green beans," says Brian. "That would be something different."

"So Beth," says Mom. "What's new?"

I hold my breath because earlier today Beth had looked in at my room, where I was working on a paper at my desk.

"Hey," she said.

"Hey," I replied.

She walked into my room and looked at my paper without seeming very interested in it. "My friend, Meredith, says that her sister kissed you the other day. Is that right?"

I'm not sure I want to have this conversation with Beth. "Maybe," I said noncommittally, like it's just too hard for me to keep track of all the girls I kiss.

"Her sister's name is Megan. Megan Boucher."

"Maybe," I said.

"Do you love her?"

"No."

"Then why did you maybe kiss her?"

It's a pretty good question, really. At some point we're going to need to demote Beth from Princess to Reporter.

"When I was doing my rounds with the paper, I came to the Bumgarner house and it turned out that Trish Bumgarner was having a slumber party with a bunch of her friends. They were a little crazy and two of them kissed me and I think one of those was Megan. I don't think it meant anything. I think it just meant that they were getting a little crazy and Trish's parents shouldn't have left them alone."

"Oh," she said and after a minute she walked away.

So now at the dinner table I'm wondering if Beth is still thinking about my loveless kiss orgy at the Bumgarners and if that will be the answer to "What's new?"

"At recess Friday we were playing Barbie tag – Meredith, Bryne, Ashleigh and me – and at the end of each game we always say Two Four Six Eight, like we do at the end of soccer games. Only when Meredith and me won, Ashleigh and Bryne said "Two – Four – Six – Eight – Who do we hate, hate, hate? Meredith and Beth. Boo!"

"That's terrible!" says Mom. "Did you say something to the teacher?"

"No," says Beth with a sigh. Of course she didn't say anything to the teacher. Mom works in an elementary school, but she doesn't seem to understand the school code of silence. You don't tell on your fellow students.

"Ashleigh's a jerk," says Brian. "Don't hang out with her."

This is pretty good advice. Ashleigh seems like a jerk to me. I'm surprised actually that she and Bryne bothered to repeat the "hate." It would have been easier to say "Two – Four – Six – Eight - Who do we hate?" Now, if Beth wanted to do a hate chant, you know she'd be sure to make the words fit the tune. She probably improved on the chant in her telling of it.

And what is Barbie tag? Maybe you say the name of a Barbie character when you're going to get tagged. Or maybe if you're tagged you get a B and then next time you get an A and when you get up to BARBIE then you're It.

"Some people just hate to lose," says Mom. "And some people think it's going to make them feel more important if they're mean to other people." We pass food around for a moment. "So what happened after that?" asks Mom.

Beth shrugs. "Spanish."

This gets Brian going. "Dos! Cuatro! Seis! Ocho! Que Odiamos? Ashleigh!"

"This is America," says Dad. "We do our hate chants in English here."

Brian reports on a choir practice where he learned about how to breathe while singing. I think *How to Breathe* might make a good sequel to *How to Pee*.

Mom tells us a story about open house at the school where she's a librarian. It's an elementary school in a pretty poor area and she was talking with an immigrant family and they had along a little girl who isn't in school yet. Mom asked the girl's name and they said "fuh-MAH-lee." Mom asked if it was a family name and the mother said, "No. They gave her the name at the hospital."

We stare at her, but none of us can figure it out.

"I was stumped for a while," she says, 'but then I asked her, 'How is the name spelled?' And the answer was F-E-M-A-L-E. The hospital had put a bracelet on the baby girl's wrist identifying her as Female then whatever the family's last name was. The family decided it was the baby's name and figured that in this country the hospitals get to name the babies."

"I think it's a pretty name," says Beth. "At least it's not Turd."

Mom told Beth once that she had considered naming her after a Norwegian cousin named Turid, which in Norway is pronounced something like "TOO-rid." It's a pretty safe bet that if she had been given that name she would have been known on the playground as Turd.

I like Beth's answer. You can't tell someone that their name is a mistake. Better just to enjoy it as a pretty name.

Mom looks at me. It's my turn to share something. "Darren?"

I study my beans and try not to think about whether or not I love Megan Boucher. "You know that meeting I went to at the Butler's last night? Well, Kyle Butler gave a long talk about why hunting is bad. Maybe he's right and maybe he's wrong. I don't know. But there's one thing that's been worrying me." I glance around the table. "He and another guy are planning to be Deerwalkers. Do you know what that is? They're planning to dress in deer colors and walk around in the woods during hunting season."

"Why?" asks Mom.

"That's crazy!" says Brian. "That's just crazy."

"I'm thinking maybe they want to get shot," I say.

Dad responds to this. "Why would they want to get shot?"

I'm not sure, but I keep talking. "They want to make a point about hunting."

"I don't like hunting," says Beth. "I think it's mean."

"The idea," I say, "is that if people know they're going to be out in the woods, it will make hunters afraid to shoot at things they think are deer since it might be a person."

"Brian's right," says Dad. "That's crazy. You ought to be able to make a point without getting yourself shot."

"We have to stop them," says Mom. "We can't let them go out and get shot."

"How?" says Dad.

"I don't care!" says Mom. "Lock them up if you have to!"

"You can't just lock up teenage boys."

This is something that happens sometimes when there's a family argument. The kids drop out while Mom gets louder and more agitated and Dad gets more contained and logical.

"You sure as [heck] can lock up teenage boys! I'd [darn] well rather lock them up than bury them!"

"I'm just saying that there might be better ways to handle the issue."

"Fine! Handle it anyway you like! But for [heaven's] sake let's do something!"

There's a long silence at this point. I decide finally that I'll try to say something more. "I saw Mrs. Butler after the meeting," I say quietly, eyes fixed on my beans. "I asked her if she was worried about Kyle's safety." I poke a bean with my fork. "What she said was *'I'm Kyle's Mom. I worry about his safety every day.'*"

"That's not much of an answer," says Mom.

"Thinking about it afterwards," I say, "I'm not positive she understands what Kyle is planning to do."

Mom looks around. "I'll call Janie – Mrs. Butler," she says. She's calm now. She has something she can do. I think about posing the question of how we should report on the story in the Tribune, but decide not to push the topic any further at dinner. We can tackle it in the Overthinking Department.

Mom takes a breath and looks at Dad then at us. "I believe Your Father has some news to share."

I'm all ears and a little nervous. I hear Mom and Dad yelling at each other sometimes late at night when they think we're all asleep. My friend Joel's parents are divorced and his Mom always refers to his Dad as 'Your Father,' like he's Lord Voldemort and you can't say his name. But Dad is smiling. "I don't know if any of you know who Charlene Chapel is, but she's an up-and-coming country singer and her next album is going to include *I Might Be in the Store But I'm Not in the Market.*"

We all clap and shout, because this is a funny song that Dad wrote.

"Hey!"

"Yay!'

"Are we rich?'

Beth stands and holds a fork to her mouth like it's a microphone and sings:

> *Just 'cause I'm a check-out girl doesn't mean I'll check out you!*
> *La-la, la-la, la-la - and my uniform is new!*
> *So stop your la-la la-la, I've got better things to do!*
> *Just 'cause I'm a check-out girl doesn't mean I'll check out you!*

At this point, Brian and I stand and join her in the chorus:

> *Oh, I might be in the store but I'm not in the market!*
> *I've heard it all before and I can tell you where to park it!*
> *That's not what I'm here for, so just give your thoughts a shove!*
> *I might be in the store but I'm not in the market-*
> *For your LOVE!*

Probably Megan Boucher doesn't know I exist. She was just caught up in showing off for her friends. Only she did have me put my hand behind her head. Also, she told her little sister that she kissed me. So she had to know my name to tell her sister, right? Why would she do that unless she wanted it to get back to me through Beth?

Now I get a little movie in my head:

> Megan and her little sister are hanging out at home and one of Megan's friends comes over. This is someone who was at the Bumgarner sleepover and she decides to tease Megan in front of her little sister.
>
> "Did Megan tell you about her new boyfriend? Her new boyfriend who's not much older than you are?"
>
> Megan tells her to cut it out, but her friend won't let up.
>
> "It's Darren McAlpine! Not Brian – Darren! He's her little pint-sized dreamboat! Last Saturday when we were at a Trish's sleepover he showed up selling newspapers and Megan gave him a great big kiss!"

I'm not saying it's a great little movie, but it seems pretty plausible to me. Meanwhile, I'm trying to write two alternatives for an editorial. I'm doing this because there's one particular meeting of the Overthinking Department that made an impression on me. Brian was asking if we should run a correction on a story we didn't quite get right and Dad said Yes.

"I knew you were going to say that," said Brian.

"Have you written a draft?" asked Dad.

"No."

"Well, if you knew what I was going to say, why didn't you go ahead and write up a draft of the correction?"

So if I think I know what Dad's going to want us to do, I want to be able to say 'OK, here it is!' What will Dad say about the Kyle Butler Deerwalker article? I'm guessing he'll say we should have an editorial to go along with the article. What should our position be? What he usually recommends is that we write up two potential editorials – one for each side of whatever the question is. Then we see which editorial makes the most sense. If it's a close call, we can always run both editorials.

So here's what I've come up with so far.

Don't Shoot

Whether you support or oppose the hunting of deer in our local forests, we all should appreciate the effort and courage that Thomson Acres high school student Kyle Butler has brought to his campaign to end the local hunting. He and his associates are studying the issue carefully and working hard to get people to think about a situation that most of us take for granted. Most dramatically - and of most concern to us at the Tribune - he and at least one of his associates have stated their intent to put their own safety and possibly their own lives on the line by being Deerwalkers. That is, they intend to dress in deer-like colors and walk in woods where deer are found during hunting season.

This is not a tactic we agree with. It is dangerous and could lead to real tragedy. No animal life is worth saving at the cost of a human life.

*However, given this situation, **we call on all deer hunters to put down their guns** until an agreement is worked out and the coast is clear. While you may have a right to hunt, all of us will be grateful for your patience in not exercising that right when our neighbors are at risk.*

Don't Be a Deerwalker

Thomson Acres high school student Kyle Butler has brought impressive effort to his campaign to end the local hunting. We salute the fact that he and his associates are working hard to get people to think about the issue. We do not salute the fact that he and at least one of his associates have stated their intent to risk their own safety and the safety of others by being Deerwalkers. That is, they intend to dress in deer-like colors and walk in woods where deer are found during hunting season.

This is a tactic that we deplore. It is dangerous and could lead to real tragedy. Differences of opinion about hunting should be settled through discussion and not through violence. This includes violence against yourself.

***We call on Kyle and his associates to put an end to the threat of Deerwalking.** We can and do request that deer hunters hold their fire until the situation is resolved and the coast is clear. However, not all hunters read this newspaper. The only sure way to avoid a tragedy is to keep the protests where they belong - on our streets and in our homes and not in the state forest during hunting season.*

The two versions are not as opposed to one another as I expected. I print out copies of my article and the two editorials and take them with me to the table in the family room. Brian is sitting there already, playing around with some clip art on his computer.

Dad comes in with a big glass of something with ice cubes in it and sits down.

"Welcome to the Overthinking Department!" he says. "Our watchword today is kiss, K-I-S-S, which stands for Keep It Simple Stupid. Which is actually four words, but we call it a watchword anyway." He wipes some liquid off the outside of his glass. "Sorry, by the way, about the Stupid. We don't mean to call names. We just needed another S for the abbreviation." He smiles and looks at us both. "Well, actually, it's more of an acronym than an abbreviation."

After a pause, Brian and I applaud.

"I love the Overthinking Department," I say.

"What's the watchword for tomorrow?" asks Brian.

"Consistency," says Dad. "So what do we have?"

"Quote with a bad joke," says Brian.

"Deerwalkers and puppies," I say.

"Urinal signage," says Dad, pulling a notecard from his pocket. "Where shall we begin?"

Brian holds up his hands. "If we put it off, I'm just going to be thinking about urinal signage. We've got to start there."

"Done," says Dad. "I don't think there's a Tribune story here, but this just seemed to me like a perfect candidate for the Overthinking Department. They installed a couple of new urinals in the men's room at the Peabody." That's the place where he performs most weeks, the Peabody Inn. It looks like a big, old-fashioned restaurant to me, but they call it an inn. I guess maybe there are hotel rooms upstairs. "There's some writing on them and I wrote it down because I wanted to get it right."

He reads from his notecard:

> *Pint Flush - saves 88% more water than a one gallon urinal.*

He turns the notecard around and sets it down on the table so we can see it. "OK, that's the statement. Does it make sense? And – I think – the more interesting question is, if it doesn't make sense, what kind of a mistake is it? Is it a math error or a grammar error?"

Brian and I stare at the card. I try not to get distracted by the relationship between a gallon and a pint. I think I see the problem. "How much water does a one gallon urinal save?" I ask.

"Ka-ching!" says Brian. "Nothing. There's no reason to think that a one gallon urinal saves any water. I mean, compared to what? So 88% more than zero would be zero. Maybe this is just a sneaky way to say the new urinal doesn't save any water."

"Uses might work," I say. "Uses 88% less water than a one gallon urinal. That would make sense, wouldn't it?"

"Or turn it around," says Brian. "Uses 12% as much water as a one gallon urinal. Is that right? Is a pint 12% of a gallon?"

This is addressed to me. Units of measure might as well be state capitals. The younger you are, the more likely you are to know them. "Two pints in a quart," I say. "Four quarts in a gallon. So eight pints in a gallon. Is that 12%?"

"Near enough," says Dad. "Math error or grammar error?"

"Oo," says Brian. "Oo-oo-oo. Saves more. Uses less. I'm thinking it's the words that got messed up and not the numbers."

"Maybe," I say. "But more versus less. That's kind of math-y. I'm not sure it's either one. Can we call it a logical error?"

"Mmm. Or maybe a marketing error," says Brian. "Somebody wants 88% and not 12% because 88% is bigger and they want More rather than Less because More sounds better, so they made up a sign that says 88% More even though it doesn't make sense."

"Marketing error it is," says Dad, putting the card back in his pocket. "Score one for the Overthinking Department. We're on a roll, but I'm not sure we're ready for Deerwalkers yet." He looks at Brian. "Bad joke?"

"Maybe-maybe. Here's the deal," he says. "Mrs. Bergstrom is always busting my chops that she doesn't get her name in the paper. So last time I saw her, she says she has a joke for me. Drumroll please:

"I love Deepwood Road. We have the Wright family next door to us and the Wong family up the street. So as our kids grow up, we've been able to teach them the difference between Wright and Wong."

"That's a pretty good joke," says Dad. "Is that right? I mean correct. Is there a Wright family and a Wong family on Deepwood Road? I know there's a Wong family."

"No," he says. "The Wongs live on Deepwood but there's no Wright family anywhere in the neighborhood."

"Bad news!" says Dad. He makes a face. "It would be better if both names were made up. Then it's just a joke. If there are real Wongs but no real Wrights then it just sounds like you're making fun of the Wongs' name."

Dad is cautious about stuff like this, and not just with the newspaper. Last night he was having a problem with Mom's idea for the movie-star-name costume party. She was thinking that she could dress up as an old-time Jewish priest with a big pair of holy dice. She was going to be Uma Thurman. (The name of the holy dice in the Old Testament isn't actually Uma Thurman, but I guess it's close enough for the purposes of the party. The country in Europe isn't actually Poor-Chagall.) Mom was thinking she might wear a robe and a fake beard and make some big dice with Hebrew characters on them.

"You can't do that," he said. "It's going to look terrible! It's going to look anti-Semitic."

"There's nothing anti-Semitic about it!" Mom said. "It's just a play on a bit of Bible trivia." But in the end Mom agreed to think of another costume.

Brian is drumming on the table. "Can't look like we're making fun of the Wongs. It's painful, though. Don't get a lot of good jokes and - like I said - Mrs. Bergstrom keeps nagging me about getting into the paper."

"Is there a way we can fix it?" I ask.

"I love Deepwood Road," says Dad. "You could end it there. I love Deepwood Road says Jeanine Bergstrom."

"I love Deepwood Road," says Brian. "The Wong family lives up the street."

'I love Deepwood Road," I say. "As our children grow up here, we can teach them - things."

Dad gets a serious look on his face. "I love Deepwood Road," he says. "It saves 88% more water than a one gallon urinal."

We sit around for a minute, waiting to see if anyone will add another one. Nobody does, so I try something else. "Maybe we could balance it off with a joke from Mrs. Wong about the Bergstroms."

We sit around for another minute. Brian speaks first. "What is thees Bergstrom?" he says in an accent I can't identify. "Eet sounds like beeg block of ice where you play gee-tar!"

Dad holds up a finger. "I love Deepwood Road," he says. We have the Bergstroms and the Strombergs. I don't know if I'm coming or going." He shrugs. "It's not much a joke, but it's very parallel."

"Could we ask the Wongs about the Wright and Wong joke?" I say. "They might think it's fine."

Brian looks at Dad, who takes a drink. "It's not fair to ask someone if something offends them. It puts them in a terrible position. Even if it does offend them, they won't want to say so. *'So, Darren. Here's this cartoon we want to run. It depicts you as a Nazi child molester. It's all in good fun, though. You aren't offended by this, are you?'* What are you going to say?"

"No mas," says Brian. "All righty. No quote from Mrs. Bergstrom this time around."

Dad looks at me. "Deerwalkers and puppies? If that's a choice, I choose puppies."

"Here's the thing," I say. "The Olsons have a new puppy. I've got a little notice about it ready to go. But why do they need a new puppy? As I was writing up the little notice, I remembered that we had a missing pet notice from the Olsons not that long ago. It seems like every week we have a missing pet notice from somebody. Have our readers ever found any of the missing pets?"

Dad and Brian look at each other. "I don't know," says Brian.

"You could do a follow-up," says Dad. "Make a list of everybody who's posted a missing pet notice over the past six months. Next time you make your rounds, ask those people if they ever found their missing pet."

Brian makes a face. "Not a happy question. A lot of people are going to say No." We sit thinking for a moment. Brian goes on. "And what are we going to do about it? If everybody says No, does that mean we're going to stop publishing missing pet notices?"

"I'd still like to know," I say. "I'll make a list. OK?"

"OK."

"Deerwalkers." I pull out my papers and look at Dad. "Did Mom talk to Mrs. Butler? And - while we're at it - is it right to call her Mrs. Butler since she has a different last name?"

"Janie Freihofer," says Dad. "But she's married to a Butler and the kids are named Butler so Yes, it's OK to call her Mrs. Butler." He takes a sip from his glass. "Mom called her last night and I'll just say that she wasn't happy about the call."

"OK," I say. "Here's a draft article I don't like and here are two different draft editorials we could run with it – if we decide to run anything on this story." I hand the article about the meeting to Dad and the two editorials to Brian. Then I sit like a doomed man while they read. They sit and read the pages I gave them and then trade the papers and read the other pages.

I try to think about something happy. Most of the time I don't remember what I dream about at night. When I do remember, my most common dream is really boring. I need to be somewhere and I can't figure out how to get there. Apparently I don't have enough time to worry about getting places when I'm awake.

Every so often I get a flying dream, which is a good dream. I don't fly like a bird or like Superman. What I can do – and it seems real enough to me that sometimes I think I really can do this – is levitate. By holding my breath in a certain way and tightening my tummy I can lift myself up and hover maybe ten or fifteen feet off the ground. I can turn around or adjust my position in the air by waving my arms and legs around like I'm swimming in the air. It's very peaceful up there and the flying comes in handy sometimes when I want to win a game of hide-and-seek or get away from bad guys.

Finally, Dad looks at Brian. "What do you think?" he says.

Brian hits his head with a fist and makes a hollow knocking sound with his tongue. "Deerwalking is crazy," he says. "It could be a three word editorial. *'Deerwalking-Is-Crazy.'* Here's the thing, though. I don't like running an editorial telling Kyle Butler what he should do. I mean, why not just call him up?"

"Good point," says Dad.

"So, Mr. Publisher," says Brian. 'What do you think?"

Dad looks back and forth at us. "Here's the question I'm wondering about. Is publicity for this thing good or bad? Does it help or hurt? Because we could ignore this story and hope it goes away or we could try to bootstrap up a lot of publicity for it." He points at Brian. "What's the Pro case for publicity?"

"Ho-kay," he says. "The Pro case is that publicity will get Deerwalkers onto people's radar screens. People includes hunters - who will either stop hunting or at least be more careful than they would have been if they hadn't heard about it."

Dad looks at me. "What's the Con case?"

"What's the Con case? The Con case is that publicity might encourage Kyle and his friends. It's sort of rewarding them for bad behavior."

Brian nods. "Or the threat of bad behavior."

"What else?" asks Dad. He gives us a moment but we just stare at him. "The other downside of publicity is that it could encourage copycats. It gives people the idea. Now instead of two crazy kids in Thomson Acres, you have lots of crazy kids all over the place."

"Not a good thing," says Brian.

"So," says Dad. "How do we weigh those things against each other? The Pro side: more people know about it, probably makes things safer for Kyle and his friend - who we should probably start naming and not just referring to as Kyle's friend. The Con side: big-time publicity could encourage other people to get shot."

"Brad," I say. "Kyle's friend is named Brad. I don't know his last name."

"What's the balance?" says Dad. "Which way do you think we should go?"

"I vote for Kyle," says Brian. "If we have to decide between Kyle's safety and the safety of other people we don't know who might live anywhere and might not even exist - even though there might be a lot of those other people, I vote for Kyle."

Dad looks at me. "Darren?"

I want to vamp for time. I could repeat the question, but it's just 'Darren?'

"I don't think one person is more important than another person just because I know them or they live in my neighborhood. But I do think a real person is more important than possible people."

Dad looks at me. "Which translates as?"

"I vote for Kyle."

"OK," says Dad. "Two votes for Kyle. Brian votes for Kyle out of neighborhood loyalty and Darren votes for Kyle out of loyalty to real rather than theoretical human beings. Votes for Kyle in this case mean that we should go for maximum publicity. Right?"

"Yes," we say.

"Well, I think so, too," he says. "But my reason is a little more mundane. If anything happens to Kyle - or his friend, Brad - your mother will kill me."

"So, what do we do?" I ask.

Dad smiles. "Welcome to the Overthinking Department!" he says. "Actually, it's not technically overthinking when you're trying to figure out how to keep people from getting shot. Then it's just the Thinking Department. How do we get publicity?" He looks at Brian and me. "Anyone?"

"We call the newspaper," says Brian. "We call the local TV news stations."

"It would be better," I say, "if Kyle was a celebrity. Maybe he's actually the son of Brad Pitt and Angelina Jolie, but he's being raised by the Butler family."

Brian cuts in: "And he and a couple of his supermodel friends are planning to Deerwalk naked."

"Deer body paint," I say.

"OK," says Dad. "Good start. How do we get people engaged? Are people going to be more engaged if we take a strong stand or less engaged?"

"More?" I say.

"Maybe," says Dad, "But maybe not. I worry that people will let us be outraged for them. Maybe if we just put it out there as information - *hey, some high school kids are planning to run around in the woods during hunting season* - maybe people will respond. Can you try that?"

We nod and grunt.

Dad takes a drink. "What I'd really like to find is somebody to push back in the other direction. Somebody other than us. Who might that be?" He looks at us.

"Hunters?" I say.

"Gun lovers?" says Brian.

"Good," says Dad. "Who else?"

We stare at him.

"Kyle's friends?" says Brian. "Kyle's family members?"

Maybe," says Dad. "Say we were the New York Times. We're covering this story. Who else do we interview?"

"The police?" I say.

"Now you're talking," says Dad.

"Yeah," says Brian. "Are they cool with Deerwalking? Are they cool even with the march? It's a story either way, but it's a better story if they aren't cool with it."

"And then," I say, "if we're the New York Times, we do a magazine piece interviewing Kyle's second grade teacher."

Brian launches into a little-old-lady falsetto. *"Little Kyle was always interposing himself. The kids would have their hands up to ask a question, and I'd try to point at Jimmy or Molly but Little Kyle would have moved himself in between so that I was accidentally pointing at him!"*

"And we get a celebrity to write an op-ed piece about Deerwalking," I say.

Brian is still doing the voice. *"Of course, he wouldn't know the answer."*

"Let's reconvene tomorrow," says Dad. "Take a look at the article and the editorials - maybe mash the editorials together. Think about who we can talk to from the police and from hunters and anywhere else. Let's call some gun rights activists. I guarantee you they'll see this as an attack on gun rights. Maybe they'll want to have a counter-demonstration. And think about stuff other than Deerwalkers, OK? Here's a homework assignment. I want the names of the next seven dwarfs. Not the First Seven Dwarfs – the Next Seven Dwarfs."

Beth yells that the phone is for me. I come to get it and she says "It's Lucille," and hands me the phone with a meaningful look that I can't quite read.

Lucille is a girl who goes to the school where Mom is librarian. Mom tries to do some stuff with her, I guess because Lucille takes an interest in the library and her home is lousy. She came along with us when we went to the fair a few weeks ago.

"Hi," she says.

"Hi."

"This is Lucille," she says. "Remember me?"

"Yeah."

"That was fun at the Big E," she says. The Big E is the name of the fair. I believe E stands for Exposition.

I don't know what to say to her. She's a year ahead of me and she's a little weird-looking and she talks in an annoying monotone. I wish her well and I'm glad Mom takes an interest in her, but I'm surprised she's calling me and I don't want to be her boyfriend.

"It was pretty fun," she says, "only you didn't win me anything."

She means I didn't win a prize at one of the game booths and then give it to her. I assume the game booths at the fair are all bogus cheats and I don't even try them. Lucille apparently really needs a guy in her life who will win a prize and give it to her.

"Yeah," I say.

"Remember when we went on the roller coaster?"

"Yeah."

"When we were on the roller coaster together, I thought about giving you a hickey."

"Oh."

"You know what a hickey is?"

"Yeah," I say. I don't know what a hickey is, but you can't admit something like that.

Lucille tells me about her neighbor's dog and the new McDonald's and the things she remembers from the fair. I hold the phone to my ear like a monkey with my hand caught in a jar. Beth from her perch in the next room has been watching me as closely as she watches *Frozen* videos, but eventually she loses interest and wanders away.

"I have to go," I say.

Lucille tells me about her favorite song.

"I have to go," I say.

"I'll call you again."

I should tell her not to call again, but I can't. It would be rude and mean to tell someone not to call again.

"Good bye."

"Good bye."

I'm not opposed in principle to getting calls from girls. I probably wouldn't mind it if pretty and popular girls my own age called me up to flirt with me, although I wouldn't know what to say to them, either.

I'm on the phone. Dad is on the other line, but only as a back-up in case of emergency. We've just been put through from the police switchboard.

"Community Relations. Officer Roger Stephenson."

"Hello," I say. "My name is Darren McAlpine. I'm deputy editor of the Thomson Acres Tribune. It's a neighborhood newspaper in the Thomson Acres neighborhood. I have a few questions I'd like to ask about, if this is a good time."

I'm thinking – *Get to the point.*

"OK," he says. "Thomson Acres Tribune. How real a paper is that?"

This seems disrespectful. If I didn't sound like a kid he probably wouldn't be asking me this question. "How real a paper?" I say. "I don't know. It's pretty real. We're in our second year."

"Here's the thing," he says. "I can't answer any questions for the press. That would need to go through our Communications Department."

Now I feel bad. I was thinking he was disrespectful but he was just trying to be helpful. And now I'm going to sound totally bogus.

"Oh," I say. "We're not the press-press. It's not really a very real paper. It's a sort of a hobby thing. I write a bunch of the paper, and I'm eleven years old. In fact, let's forget about the paper. I have some questions that I'm interested in as a resident of my neighborhood. OK?

"Sure," he says. "Happy to help if I can."

"Great. Thanks. We have some local young people who are planning some protests about deer hunting. The first thing is a protest march. They're planning to march up Hipkins Road from the Thomson Acres sign to the parking lot for the reservoir and state forest. Does the police have any issue with a march like that?"

"Well, that depends," he says. "How many people are expected?"

"I don't know."

"Do you have a guess?"

"I don't know."

"More than fifty?"

"No."

"Are they planning to block traffic?"

"No."

"OK," he says. "Here's the deal. For a big march, something that might disrupt traffic, they should get a permit. When you have protesters who want to block traffic, we like to know ahead of time so that we can have a response ready. Otherwise – if it's just a small group of people marching along the side of the road – we don't need to be involved."

"Oh."

"They could request a police escort, but it probably won't happen unless they want to pay for it."

"Oh," I say. "Thank you. There's something else. After hunting season opens, some of them are talking about dressing up in neutral colors and walking around in the woods so that hunters will have to be careful to avoid shooting them."

"They're talking about what?"

"They call it Deerwalking," I say. "Instead of wearing a red hat or an orange vest, they try to blend in and walk around where the deer might be. I believe it's intended to discourage people from hunting."

"Sounds dangerous."

"Is it illegal? Might the police stop them?"

"I might have to get back to you on that," he says. "We don't usually get involved in enforcing hunting laws. Mostly that falls to the D.E.E.P."

The D.E.E.P.?" I say.

"The state Department of Energy and Environmental Protection. Would you like their number?"

"That's OK," I say. "One more question. Say I'm a hunter. I go out to shoot a deer and by mistake I end up shooting one of these Deerwalking protesters. Do you get involved then, or is that also the D.E.E.P.?"

"It actually depends where the shooting takes place. Most of the deer hunting takes place in the state forest. If somebody got shot there, the state police would normally be the ones to investigate."

"Oh," I say. "Thanks."

"So, does that answer your questions?"

"Yes."

"You be safe, OK?"

Our next call is to the offices of the Brad Pincher Show. It's a daytime talk radio show in the region. We're thinking he might have a reaction to Deerwalking because one of the issues he likes to talk about is gun rights. The Brad Pincher website has a link to a site called GunsMakeUsSafer.com. We get connected to a producer named Mr. Blake.

"Good afternoon. My name is Darren McAlpine, and my brother and I produce a neighborhood newspaper in the Thomson Acres section of Canton. As you may know, there's a pretty big state forest near here and deer hunting season starts up in another week or two. One thing that's happening this year is that some young people who oppose deer hunting are planning a protest."

"They oppose deer hunting?" he asks.

"Yes they do. I believe their position is that hunting is cruel to the deer and not the best way to control the deer population."

"And what do they propose instead?"

"Actually, before we get into that, what I want to ask you about is the protest. They're doing the things you might expect – holding a meeting and organizing a march. But they're also planning something else that you might not expect. Some of them are planning to go out in the woods during hunting season and walk around without wearing any bright colors or doing anything else to warn hunters that they're there. They call it Deerwalking."

"I don't understand," he says. "What's the point?"

"The point is that the hunters will have to be extra careful in order to make sure they only shoot deer and don't accidentally shoot one of the protesters. I suppose if one of the protesters did get shot, he would end up being a kind of martyr for the cause."

I'm not sure what's happening, but then I realize that he's laughing. "That is the stupidest thing I've ever heard in my life! Oh, man! What do they call it when people get themselves killed doing stupid things? The Darwin Awards?"

"Do you have a comment for us?"

"A comment? I'm going to talk to Brad about this. We could do a whole show on this story. Send me what you've got on this thing. I don't want people thinking that we just made it up. It's perfect! It's a perfect metaphor for what's happening with all the anti-gun forces in this country. They want to get us all killed, and I guess they've decided to start with themselves."

Afterwards, Dad says, "A martyr for the cause?"

"Too much?" I say.

"No, it was good. You held your ground with a grown-up. You pushed his buttons."

"Thanks," I say. "But you know grown-ups are mostly pretty nice. It's kids who are impossible. We have this bogus sixth grade newsletter and I was supposed to get a quote from Keenan Avery about some skiing award he won and all he would say is "This sucks!" and the "The newsletter sucks" and "You suck." He knows they won't print any of that in the newsletter."

"So what did you do?"

"I said to him, 'How about if we say you said this?' And then I gave him a quote that was like: *'I'm so honored to win this award!'* and he said OK, so that was his quote."

Dad gives me a funny smile. He says, "Journalism is a dirty business sometimes."

Here are the revised drafts for the newspaper that I came up with, with some help from Brian.

"I Don't Want to Get Shot!"

Local Student Ready to Risk Life for Deer

Last Thursday evening, eleven high school students from the area gathered at the Butler's house on Glenview Road to hear Kyle Butler make a presentation about deer hunting. Butler opposes hunting deer for a variety of reasons, which he explained in some detail. He invited those who share his concerns to participate in a march on October 17 from the Thomson Acres sign to the state forest parking lot. The march will start at noon.

Butler also said that he and a classmate, Brad Desjardins, are planning to be "Deerwalkers." This means that they will wear deer-colored clothing and walk as close to deer as they can in the state forest during hunting season. They hope that their presence will discourage hunters from shooting at the deer.

When asked about the possibility that he could be shot by hunters, Butler replied, "I don't want to get shot, but I also want to change this situation."

Please see the accompanying editorial.

Brave Stand or Dangerous Stunt?

We support the right of all people to speak their minds and lead non-violent protests when they want to make a point. But is it fair and appropriate for area young people to protest deer hunting by making themselves human targets?

Is this a brave stand or a dangerous stunt?

*Please let us know what **you** think. Call our number or send us an email to give us your vote. Give us whatever comments you might have. We'll share your input in our next issue.*

The Next Seven Dwarfs

Blinky, Cheeky, Frumpy, Sloppy, Wheezy, Woozy and Mumbles.

I think my Dwarfs list is pretty negative until I see Brian's list, which is:

Next Seven Dwarfs

Dumpy, Icky, Greasy, Tacky, Flabby, Whiny and Dork.

I'm reading in bed and Mom looks in on me. "Darren, could you come to the dining room for a minute?"

I'm suddenly scared and alert. What's going on? I put on a robe and go to the dining room, where Brian is already sitting in his robe, eating a plate of cucumbers.

He has this snack he likes to make where he'll peel a cucumber and cut it up into little chunks and cover them with Italian salad dressing. This is Exhibit A of what happens when kids get too old for their own good. Their senses start to dull. My senses are still young and sharp enough to know that cucumbers - with or without salad dressing - are very nasty-tasting.

Mom and I sit at the table. Dad is off performing. Beth, I assume, is in bed asleep. Mom speaks quietly.

"This has been a hard week for your sister," she says, "and things aren't going to get any easier for her."

"Is this about her doctor shoes?" I ask.

Beth has some issue with her feet. The doctor prescribed special shoes for her and they arrived this week. They look like Darth Vader shoes - big, black clodhopper shoes, almost like ski boots. Beth is used to wearing delicate, little princess shoes. For a long time, she would only wear shoes that lit up when she took each step.

Beth is supposed to wear the doctor shoes a certain number of hours each day. She hates the shoes and only puts them on when forced to and takes them off as soon as she can get away with it. You'd think they were hurting her, but I don't think they do. She probably just hates them because of how they look.

Eventually, Beth is going to have to wear the doctor shoes to school. This is maybe a week away, and it has been hanging over her head like a death sentence.

"Yes," says Mom. "It's about the doctor shoes. She needs to wear them so her feet grow right, but she really, really hates those shoes."

"Ya think?" says Brian.

"Yes, I think - and your Dad and I would appreciate it if you guys could find ways to help her feel better."

"Like what?" says Brian.

"Well, for one thing, tell her she looks nice. Don't make fun of her when she's wearing the shoes. And don't start humming the Darth Vader music when she walks into the room."

"Ouch," I say. Brian was the one who had hummed the song earlier that evening, but I had thought it was pretty funny at the time.

"This is important," says Mom. "She needs to get her arches shaped right while her feet are still growing. She doesn't need to take a lot of B.S. from her own family about it."

"Got it," says Brian. "How long is she going to have to wear those things?"

"Not her whole life, but for a while. Maybe six months with the full boots. Maybe another six months with smaller boots. Maybe what they call orthotics inserted into regular shoes after that. It's going to be a long, tough haul for her."

"The boots - do they only come in black?" asks Brian.

"Black, white or purple," says Mom. "We gave her the choice. She picked black."

"Could we decorate them somehow?" I ask.

"Maybe," says Mom. "She hasn't seemed very interested in the topic. Maybe she's afraid that decoration will just draw attention to them. Maybe that's why she picked the black ones."

Brian takes a bite of cucumber. "So - what if Darren and I started wearing boots like that. Would that help?"

I'm thinking: Is he crazy? Why would we wear clodhopper Darth Vader boots just to make our sister feel better? Because you know it wouldn't be enough to wear them around the house. She has to wear them to school, so we'd have to wear them to school. And who at school would know that we were wearing stupid-looking boots because we were nice brothers? Probably about 1% of the people. The other 99% see a guy who's already on the cusp of dorkdom seal the deal by parading around in Dork Boots.

"I don't know," says Mom. "It's a nice thought. We had to special order those boots and they cost a fortune."

Brian shrugs and spears some more nasties. "Maybe we could find something similar-looking."

I'm thinking: Give it a rest. We have an out. The boots are special-order and expensive.

"That's actually a really nice thought," says Mom. "Maybe we can go shopping this week. In the meanwhile, please try to be supportive. OK? Capeesh?"

"Got it," says Brian.

"Got it," I say.

I like the number eleven. Two ones seems like the perfect number. Snake eyes. I think it's a good age. Solidly into double figures but not yet on the slippery edge of being a teenager.

One other thing I like about eleven is that it sounds like elven. The elves are very cool and live forever.

This'll be my last all-one age until I turn 111. It would be the coolest of all if I could live to 1,111. The next year, I wouldn't write my age as 1,112. I'd take the four ones and write a diagonal line across them.

My Mom says this should be a good year for me in school because élève is French for student, so I'm really a student-year-old. I like the idea of secret meanings in words, but it's one of those things like an action movie plot that you don't want to think about too carefully. The whole idea of a word is that people know what it means.

When I get home from school, there's a message on the answering machine.

> *"Yo Dalrymple! Check out the website. Guns Make Us Safer Dot Com. O.K. Later!"*

The lead story on the site has the headline:

Stupidest Anti-Gun Protest Ever!

The story doesn't have the kind of professional tone that we try to use at the Tribune. It also seems to be confused about whether Deerwalking is meant to protest guns or hunting. Still, we wanted to generate media coverage, and here it is. The story even credits the Thomson Acres Tribune as the source of the information.

There's a way to leave comments. I want to offer some corrections, but instead I post the following:

> *Thanks for the shout-out to the Thomson Acres Tribune. Darren McAlpine, Deputy Editor*

Journalism is a dirty business sometimes.

After dinner, I look in on Brian, who is sitting at the computer. Beth is in her room, so I keep my voice down.

"I don't want to wear Darth Vader boots," I say.

"Huh?"

"We didn't really get to talk about this the other night," I say, "but I don't want to wear Darth Vader boots."

He looks up and gives me a Mr. Innocent face. "Oh? Why not?"

"Because they look ridiculous. Will we have to wear them to school? Maybe you're cool enough to get away with wearing ridiculous boots to school, but I'm not. I show up at school in a pair of those boots and it's like Mom pinned a note to my jacket saying, 'Please beat up my kid.'"

He stands and stretches. "Deep breath in," he says. "Hold it. Hold it. Deep breath out. Don't trust your first instinct on this. Give it a minute." He looks around. "What I'm thinking is partly about Beth. Look how much you don't want to wear those boots. She's a girl. Think how much she doesn't want to wear those boots. But also, partly, I'm thinking about Skyler Franklin's friend. Know who Skyler is?"

I shake my head no.

"A kid in my class. His friend goes to Adams and is one of three brothers. One of the brothers got some kind of cancer and was on this medicine that made all his hair fall out, so the other brothers shaved their heads. Their way of showing solidarity with their brother. And Skyler's friend who shaved his head for his brother - he became like a celebrity in his class. The girls all fell in love with him."

"I don't know," I say. "Those boots."

"Hey-hey-hey: Skyler's friend," he says. "Shaved his head and the girls all fell in love with him. Plus, there's Beth."

"I'll think about it," I say.

The next afternoon, I'm on the phone taping an interview with Brad Pincher. He has an interesting voice that slides around like a trombone. Brian is listening on the other line for moral support.

I take a breath. One of the reasons I wanted to be a newspaper reporter in the first place is that I would rather be the one asking the questions.

"So, Darren. Is it OK if I call you Darren?"

"Sure," I say.

"Darren was the person who put me onto the gun protesters who are planning to walk around in the woods during hunting season and see if they can get themselves shot. Isn't that right?"

"Yeah. Sort of."

"Darren runs a neighborhood newspaper out in Canton. Very enterprising of you."

"Actually," I say, "my brother, Brian, is the editor. I'm the deputy editor."

"You're doing a great job out there. How old are you?"

"Eleven."

"Great. Now, you aren't going to be one of these walk-with-the-deer people are you, Darren?"

"No, sir. This isn't my protest. I just write about it."

"Did you hear that, ladies and gentlemen? That's journalism. Here's an eleven-year-old kid who knows the difference between writing about a protest and being a part of the protest himself. Man, don't you wish the liberal media could do that?"

"I'm sorry. Is that a question?"

"Not really, Darren. I was just making a point. It's what we call a 'rhetorical question'."

(I know what a rhetorical question is. In fact, *"Is that a question?"* was my own rhetorical question.)

"So," I say, "are you planning to organize a counter-protest?"

"We might. Lots of people who listen to this show care very deeply about this country and are willing and able to get out and let their voices be heard. What kind of protest would you recommend?"

"I'm thinking that's a trick question," I say.

"How so, Darren?"

"It's just that just a minute ago, you were saying how great it is that I just write about protests and don't try to interfere."

He laughs. "Fair enough. Maybe that was a trick question. If so, you passed. I'll know better than to try any more trick questions on you. So here's a more serious question."

"O.K."

"If these walking-with-the-deer guys get their way and shut down deer hunting in Connecticut - what do you think they'll shut down next?"

"I don't know."

"Well," he says, "here's what I think. If they shut down deer hunting in Connecticut they'll shut down deer hunting in the rest of New England and then the rest of the East Coast and then maybe the Midwest and the Far West and the South. And once deer hunting is history, they'll want to shut down bear hunting and duck hunting and any other kind of hunting. And then maybe it'll be time to shut down fishing. Although, that would make a pretty interesting picture - a bunch of crazy protesters swimming around in lakes and rivers trying to bite on hooks!"

I know I'm running out of time. I say, "The Deerwalkers are leading a protest march next Saturday at noon."

"Maybe some of my callers will have a suggestion on this when we come back. Thanks for your time today, Darren."

"Thank you."

Brian comes around the corner and gives me a high five. "Yes!" he says. "You should be in politics."

"Thanks."

"Of course," he says, "there was that moment when you lapsed into Just Talk."

"Huh?"

He starts doing a funny voice that I guess is supposed to be me. "It's just that I just think that you just shouldn't just say just things just like just that!"

"All right! All right!" I say. "Just stop it!"

"So," he says, "how do you feel?"

"A little pumped up," I say. "But also a little yucky."

"Because?"

"Because it's phony. And then he starts saying *'Isn't it wonderful, ladies and gentlemen, that this fine, young man just wants to cover the news and not influence events?'* when the whole reason I'm talking to him is to try to influence the events. I mean, that's just weird."

"I know, I know," he says. "Hopefully it's for a good cause. Dad thinks publicity might help, and Dad hasn't been wrong about anything for days now."

Other Darren is bummed out. We're in my backyard, throwing a football back and forth.

"I don't know," he says. "I don't understand it. Doug and Jamal ditched me on the way home from school."

"They ditched you?" I ask.

"Yeah. We usually walk together. B.S. about whatever's going on. Today, they had some plan or signal or something and the next thing I knew they were running around a corner and they were gone. They ditched me."

I want to give him some good advice about this, but I can't think of any.

"Maybe they had to be somewhere," I say. "It probably doesn't mean anything."

"I don't know. It means at least that they don't like walking home with me."

"Did they say anything?"

"No."

"What about last time you guys walked home together. Anything come up?"

He thinks about this. "Not really. They were pretty annoying, actually. They kept razzing me about the 'horse from the fair' thing."

He's referring to an incident in his class that I didn't see but I've heard about. Other Darren got up to give an oral report to the class, but he was having trouble with his voice because the day before he'd gone to the Big E and I guess had done a lot of running around and shouting. So he said: *"Excuse me. I'm a little hoarse from the fair."*

And some people started laughing and one of his classmates said: *"Is that true, Darren? Are you a little horse from the fair?"*

And Other Darren didn't pick up on the joke and said: *"Yes. That's why my voice is like this. It's because I'm a little hoarse from the fair."*

"It was like two weeks ago!" he says, pacing again.

There's something irresistible about the story. Even Beth will sometimes ask Other Darren if he's a little horse from the fair. I need to try a different tack.

"Girls do this kind of stuff all the time," I say. "They turn on one another. It's like they're practicing to be on some kind of reality TV show."

This is pretty true, at least among the girls at my school. There's a transitive property to female friendship. If I'm a girl and I'm Charlene's friend and Charlene doesn't like Shawna, then I don't like Shawna. If I start hanging out with Shawna, then Charlene kicks me out of her crew.

The boys don't roll that way. If I don't like Connor, that just means I'm not going to hang out with him. I don't care if Other Darren hangs out with him or not.

He stands there holding the football and looks at me. "So what does that mean?"

"I don't know. I guess it means that Doug and Jamal were being kind of girlish."

"Yeah?"

"Yeah. And you can tell them I said that – as long as they promise not to beat me up."

And – maybe to compensate for making a joke about getting beat up – I crank up and throw the football too far. Other Darren jumps, but just bumps it with his hands and it goes over the back fence. If it had gone straight back over the back fence, it would be easy to get from the Schipke's yard. Instead it went diagonally into Mr. Johnson's yard. Mr. Johnson seems pretty mean and there's no easy way to climb into his yard.

Other Darren and I go out to the street, walk around to Mr. Johnson's house and ring his doorbell. He opens the door and looks at us. I'm not sure if he knows who I am. He's on Brian's route and I don't think he ever buys a paper. I figured he would say Hi or something, but he doesn't.

"Hi," I say. "Sorry to bother you. I'm Darren McAlpine. I live around on Glenbrook. Our backyard is diagonal to yours." I try to make a diagram with my hands, but it's not very good. It's a good thing I'm not deaf. I'd be terrible at sign language.

Mr. Johnson looks over at Other Darren and back to me. He still doesn't say anything.

I continue. "We were playing with a football in our backyard and I threw it too far..."

"It was my fault," says Other Darren. "I should have caught it."

"Anyway, it went over the fence into your yard. We're sorry about it and I'm wondering if we could please get the football back."

He looks at Other Darren and he looks at me. "Whose football is it?" he asks.

"Mine," I say.

He shakes his head. "It's mine now."

He starts to close the door. "Sir!" I say. "Please! I'm really sorry. It won't happen again. I'd really like my football back."

The door is halfway shut. "You want your football back?" he says to me.

"Yes."

"Come back tomorrow," he says and closes the door.

We've been trying to find someone from a group that advocates more gun control to provide the other side of the spectrum from Brad Pincher. We're going for a three-ring circus. Kyle and his friends protesting against deer hunting, the Pincher people protesting against Kyle and his friends and then some other group protesting against Pincher.

Brian tracked down a local contact for an organization with the website repealthesecondamendment.org. So today, he's on the phone and I'm listening in the next room.

"Good afternoon, Mr. Cernak. My name is Brian McAlpine. I'm Editor of a neighborhood newspaper called the Thomson Acres Tribune."

"Sure. Thomson Acres. Out by Canton."

"That's right."

"I live in Avon. Not too far away."

"Great. Anyhoo – we've been following a story about some young people in our area who oppose deer hunting. They're planning some protests. One of the protests they're planning is something they call Deerwalking. This means that some of the protesters will walk in the woods during hunting season wearing clothes that blend into the woods."

"This isn't our protest. You know that, right? Our organization isn't opposed to legal hunting. That isn't what we're about."

"O.K."

"Some people say we're looking to take away everybody's hunting rifles and stuff. That isn't true at all."

It's a lot more relaxing listening to an interview like this than being the one who has to ask the questions.

"Yeah," says Brian. "We thought it might be good to ask you to comment. This is a story that has captured the attention of what you might call gun-rights organizations. Brad Pincher did a feature on it on his radio show and there's talk that some of his listeners will stage their own protest when the hunting protesters have their march on Saturday of next week."

"What did you say the protesters are going to do?"

"During hunting season they're threatening to have protesters walking around in the forest in order to discourage the hunters."

"How does that discourage the hunters?"

"What they're thinking - what they're hoping - is that the hunters will feel they need to be very cautious to avoid accidentally shooting one of the protesters."

"This isn't us, all right? It's not our protest. Personally, I don't even understand it."

"The other protesters, the Brad Pincher listeners, see the Deerwalking as a threat to the free exercise of their gun rights. They believe that if any anti-hunting protesters get shot, it's their own fault and there should be complete immunity for all hunters."

Brian is really leaning on the Brad Pincher angle. He must think that's the key to getting a reaction from this guy. Dad will sometimes use the expression 'a drinking game'. The idea is that people would take a drink each time a certain word is said. Today's game would be to take a drink every time Brian says 'Brad Pincher'.

"Look," says the man on the phone. "Obviously we see the world a lot differently than Brad Pincher or the NRA see it. But this is not our protest. We aren't concerned about guns that kill deer. We're concerned about guns that kill people."

"So you agree with Brad Pincher about this?"

"I don't know. Maybe. Hey. A stopped clock is right twice a day. Sorry if that disappoints you. I assume it would be more interesting for the news to have competing demonstrations shouting at each other."

The man doesn't seem to be taking the bait. Is that going to be it?

"Actually, you know what would make a good news story?" Clearly Brian has thought of some other angle to try. "If you and the Brad Pincher organization - mortal enemies from opposite ends of the gun control debate, right? - if you together were able to release a joint statement about the proposed Deerwalking protest. That would be news."

"It's an interesting idea. I doubt the Pincher people would buy it. They want all the enemies they can gin up."

"Give us a day to work on this. I know a guy who might be able to make this happen. Thanks for your time today."

After I hang up, I look in on Brian. "Plan B, I guess," I say. "You know a guy?"

He flashes me a big grin. "Sure! I'm looking at him"

I'm back at Mr. Johnson's door. Once again, I need to speak first.

"Good afternoon. Sorry to disturb you. You said I could come back today for my football."

"*Your* football?"

At first I don't know what he means, but then I remember that he said it was now his football. "Or your football," I say.

He holds up a finger and closes the door. I stand there for a few minutes wondering if that was the end of the conversation. Then he opens the door and hands me a paper bag that I can tell doesn't have a football in it.

"What's this?" I ask.

He nods to me and I open the bag. It is the charred remains of my football.

"Didn't last long in the pellet stove," he says.

I can't think of anything to say. I can't believe he did this to my football.

"You can keep it," he says. "Try to be more careful from now on."

3. Two Good Electric Sanders Ruined

I'm not sure how it's come to this, but I'm following Kyle and Brad through the woods. From the back, it looks like they're dressed up for a Christmas party. They're wearing sweaters with complicated decorations and they both have reindeer-antler gizmos clipped onto their heads. As we all run through narrow pathways, I hear the jingle bells on their antlers and also clip-clopping like we're in a Monty Python movie and somebody's running after us with coconut shells. We stop. In a clearing just ahead of us, there's a big, insurance-commercial deer with antlers. From behind us, in the bushes somewhere, comes a voice on a loudspeaker:

"This is Deer Hunting Party Number Three, preparing to shoot! If you know any reason why we should not shoot, you should immediately contact us at 1-800-DONTSHOOT. That toll-free number, once again, is 1-800-DONTSHOOT."

Stupid pod! Why couldn't I have a real phone?

I hold my breath and tense my tummy and start to lift off the ground. But I can't levitate as high as I want. Something is stopping me. Maybe I'm hitting the tree branches overhead. This isn't a good situation! Lord Jesus, Son of God, have mercy on me, a sinner.

BANG! BANG-BANG!

I don't feel anything, but I see the news story.

'DEER WALKING' HAS TRAGIC END: LOCAL BOY SHOT

(Not 'neighborhood news reporter' even though that's clearly what I was doing at the time. Not even 'area youth' which might suggest someone who's at least in double figures.)

> *The controversial tactic of 'deer walking' took its first local victim yesterday with the shooting death of Darren Mcalpine of Glenbrook Drive.*

(Hello! The 'A' should be capital. Some kid gets shot, at least spell his name right. And it's Glenbrook Road, not Drive.)

> *The shots were fired by Mr. Frank Gardenia, a real estate developer from Brookfield.*

(So the guy who shoots me gets more respectful billing than I do?)

> *"I was just trying to shoot a deer," said Mr. Gardenia. "There was a big, ten-point buck and this kid managed to get in the way." Mr. Gardenia went on to say, "That kid jumped up really high. I've never seen anything like it. He should have been in the Olympics."*

> *A spokesman for the American Hunters Club said, "We have reason to believe that the deceased individual was a member of the Deerwalkers terrorist group, whose stated purpose is to deny all Americans their Second Amendment rights. We do not believe he should be allowed to be made into a martyr by his own reckless acts of trespassing and criminal interference."*

> *"I'll never love another boy again," said tearful area youth, Megan Boucher.*

(Flipping back in the paper, I'm gratified to see that my parents have run the obituary I wrote for myself, complete with the broccoli joke, which seems pretty cool under the circumstances. Really, who could blame Megan Boucher for never loving another boy again? I feel a wave of good feeling. It could be the start of Heaven, but more likely it's that moment of relief when I can tell it's just a bad dream and it will soon be over.)

On the road again. I'm suited up in my sports coat and I've got a shoulder bag full of the latest issue of the Tribune. I'm not crazy about the wishy-washy non-editorial - *"Tell us what YOU think!"* - but I'm willing to give it a chance. We've even put a stuffer into the paper - a business-card piece of paper asking for comments on the Deerwalking question and providing contact information.

I think I look OK in the coat with the bag over my shoulder, but it isn't a look I'd try at school. I'm sometimes called "gay" at school by larger and older boys, but that's just their way of calling me a dork. I'm short, skinny and baby-faced. Also, the way I talk is probably going to remind someone more of their eccentric aunt than of Arnold Schwarzenegger.

So, yes a dork - but a dork who likes girls. Of course, we'll have to see when I grow up if a woman will ever want to marry me. My fallback position is to become a monk. I'm already an acolyte, so I'm basically halfway there. I've already got the outfit and the moves.

BING-BONG!

Mrs. DiFuria answers the door, which I take to be a good sign. She's looking good, and has some kind of handkerchief tied around her hair. Why doesn't Mrs. DiFuria have a daughter? Man, if she had a daughter in my grade, I'd think about calling her up every night.

"Good morning," I say. "New edition of the paper. Big story about hunting protests. We're asking everybody to call or email and tell us what you think. There's a card inside."

"Uh-huh," she says. "Just a second." She disappears, and I wonder if I said something wrong. Should I have said 'Good morning, Mrs. DiFuria'?

She comes back and hands me a dollar. I give her a paper and change.

"So, what do you think?" she says.

I don't know what she means. "What do I think?"

"About the hunting question."

"Oh. Right. I think the marches and the meetings are fine and probably a good thing, but the stuff about going out into the woods during hunting season is too dangerous and not really fair."

"Thanks," she says. "I'll take a look." And she waves and closes the door.

I'm mostly relieved as I head on to the Carlsens. I could have frozen up or said something really stupid. Sometimes just not being an idiot can feel like success.

The chair is gone from the Carlsen front yard, but in its place is a dog. It's a medium sized and athletic looking dog with a mottled coat that looks like its fur was stitched together from two non-matching dogs. The dog's collar has an improvised chain that is looped around the lightpost that stands halfway between the house and the street. The dog takes an immediate interest in me and comes as far in my direction as its chain allows.

"Good boy," I say. "I'm just delivering the paper."

I angle around towards the front door, but the chain is long enough that I can't get to the door without passing through the dog's space. The dog follows me step for step. I can't tell if it thinks I look like a fun visitor or a delicious snack. I circle around in the opposite direction but eventually stop when once again I can't get any closer to the door without passing into the dog's space. If I could get it to go around in circles, eventually its chain would wind around the lightpost and be short enough so that I could get to the door. But I can't get it to go around in circles. I can just get it to go one way and then the other.

This makes me think about Mrs. Featherstone, my math teacher. We did a geometry unit and one of the concepts she taught us was dimensions. A line is one dimensional. A square is two dimensional. A cube is three dimensional. Right? Only one of the sneaky details is that a line is one dimensional even if it bends. You'd think a bent line might be two dimensional since it could have a length and a width, but no. As long as you could straighten it out, the line could have a thousand bends like a ball of string and it's still a one dimensional line. So one of the questions on the test is how many dimensions does a ball of string have? And I say three dimensions, because I know that the ball of string example about the bent-up line is just an example. String isn't a line. But my answer is marked wrong, and when I ask about it Mrs. Featherstone doesn't listen to me. She just repeats the story about the bent-up line.

Not that I'm wanting to draw a direct comparison, but Ms. Jackson does listen to me. When I pointed out typos in the messages she was asking us to bring home (*"Its time for our annual Halloween Party!"*) she was very nice about it, and she now has me copy edit all her handouts.

If the Carlsen dog wrapped its chain around the lightpost, I wonder if Mrs. Featherstone would consider the chain a one dimensional object. Maybe if Mrs. Featherstone could see the dog chain wrapped around the lightpost she would realize how three dimensional it is and rethink her position on the ball of string. I think about Dad's urinal question: Is this an error in math or an error in language? Mrs. Featherstone is looking at something - string - that is an image or a metaphor for a line. She's confusing the image with the thing behind the image. Maybe it's an error in theology.

I walk back and forth a couple more times and decide to continue on to Mrs. Everett and try the Carlsens later.

"Hello?"

I look back. Mr. Carlsen is standing at the door, looking at me. I head back in his direction.

"Good morning!" I say. "Thomson Acres Tribune. New edition. Big story about hunting protests."

I stop. I've reached the point where I need to cross inside the dog's circle.

"New dog!" I say.

"Yes," says Mr. Carlsen. "Butchie." I continue standing where I am while Butchie is poised either to greet or devour me. Mr. Carlsen makes no move to help me out.

"Does he bite?" I ask.

"It's a she."

"Oh."

"Here, Butchie!" he says.

The dog stays fixed on me like I'm magnetic. I don't know why Mr. Carlsen doesn't want to come out into his front yard. He has clothes on.

"Here, Butchie, Butchie!" he says. Then he looks over at me. "She's really very sweet, as far as we can tell so far."

This doesn't convince me to step into the dog's circle. I stay put and hold up a copy of the paper aimed towards Mr. Carlsen. "New edition. I could leave it in your mailbox if you're interested. You could pay me next time."

"Sure," he says. "We're number 34."

"I know," I say. I open up the paper and take out the stuffer card. I hold it up like the Statue of Liberty. "See this?"

"Yeah."

"We're asking everyone to give us their opinion about the hunting protests. A couple of high school kids are planning to do something called Deerwalking. This card has the information for giving us a call or an email to tell us what you think. The information is also in the paper, but the card is a kind of reminder. We'll report on the results next week."

"Don't know anything about it," he says.

"OK if we put something in the paper about your new dog?" I ask.

"No," he says. "That'd be like taking out an ad asking somebody to steal her." He waves and shuts the door.

"Good Butchie!" I say to the dog and head back towards Mrs. Everett's house.

I find it annoying when people don't want to share their news. Is it such a risk to tell the neighborhood you have a new dog? Although, it's true that sometimes pets disappear and nobody knows what happened to them. The Carlsens don't have a great track record with their pets, so maybe he's not being totally crazy.

"Oh, hello!" says Mrs. Everett. "I heard you on the radio the other day. Just a moment." She disappears, leaving the door cracked open, but then she immediately reappears. "Can I show you something?"

"Sure," I say.

She leads me to a living room. "Wait just a minute please. Feel free to sit down."

She heard me on the radio? It seems impossible. I'm not sure what seems more unlikely: the fact that they broadcast that interview or the fact that Mrs. Everett listens to Brad Pincher.

I look around. Mrs. Everett's living room is pretty much what I was expecting, with one big exception. Nice, old-fashioned looking furniture, lots of little knick-knacks and a giant Abraham Lincoln statue sitting on one end of the couch. I don't sit down.

Mrs. Everett comes back down the hall carrying some kind of scrapbook or photo album. "I know you have your route. This won't take a minute."

"What's this?" I ask, pointing at Lincoln.

She stops and looks up. "What?"

"You have a giant Abraham Lincoln in your living room!"

"Oh, yes. Of course. My son is an artist. He's mostly making abstract sculpture now."

"The statue is sitting on the couch!" I say. "That's so cool!"

It is cool. You expect a statue to be on some kind of base or stand. This statue seems to be making itself at home, sitting on Mrs. Everett's couch. It's at least life size and maybe bigger than life size. It looks huge.

"Jimmy thought it would be a good fit. He had to reinforce the couch underneath. It's a very heavy thing. Here, I'll show you something." She walks past the statue and reaches down to a switch on the end table. She twists the switch and Lincoln's big hat lights up from inside.

"Wow!" I say. "Wow!"

"I guess it's pretty different," she says. "Just between you and me it takes up a lot of space. I'm glad you like it. What I was going to show you was this." And she opens up the scrapbook and holds it out to me. It's opened to a page with a photo of a girl maybe Beth's age holding a dog that looks like a beagle. "I don't know if you remember Punkin?"

Punkin was a dog that Mrs. Everett had forever. I think Punkin was probably a beagle, although she was so old when I knew her that she didn't look like much of anything except old. "Yes," I say. "I remember Punkin."

"Well this is Brenna, my granddaughter, Colleen's daughter, and their family got this beagle that looks just like Punkin did in her heyday and they call her Punkin Two. I thought that was very sweet."

"It's very cute," I say. I'm not crazy about saying the word 'cute,' but I figure it's better than repeating the word 'sweet.' I like dogs but other people's dogs aren't as interesting as your own dog. What I really want is to take a picture of Abraham Lincoln sitting on the couch. I want to take two pictures: one of Abe by himself for a feature story in the paper and a selfie of me and Abe sitting on the couch together. I'm worried though about hurting Mrs. Everett's feelings.

"Would it be OK if I take a picture of this picture?" I ask. I don't really want a picture of the girl with Punkin Two, but I figure that's the best way to start. I ask to take a picture of what she wanted to show me and then it's easier to ask to take the pictures that I really want. I'm not sure if this is being polite or sneaky.

"Why sure," she says. "That would be fine."

So I set the scrapbook down on the coffee table and pull out my pod and take a picture of the picture of Mrs. Everett's granddaughter with Punkin Two.

Whenever I start taking pictures, I ask myself: What is the Money Shot? That is, what picture would be the best possible illustration of the story? Say the story is two brothers who come in first and second in a race. For that story, the Money Shot might be a good, close-up picture of the two brothers together, holding whatever medal or trophy they each won.

I hand the scrapbook back to Mrs. Everett. "And let me get a picture of you holding the picture." It takes a minute to get things arranged so that I can see Mrs. Everett's face in the same frame with the Punkin Two photo, but that's the Money Shot.

"And would it be OK if I took a picture of the Abraham Lincoln statue?"

"Of course," she says.

"Could you turn the light out in his hat?" I ask. I'm not Mr. Photographer, but I know it's hard to get a good picture when you're shooting towards a light.

"I was going to turn it off anyway."

So I take one shot of the statue from across the room and then I sit down on the couch and take the selfie of me with Abe. All the time I'm feeling pretty cheesy. The photos of Punkin Two probably won't even come out. It's hard to take a good picture of a picture.

There's one more step left. I walk back to Mrs. Everett. "Would it be all right with you if we put something in the paper about either or both of these items?"

She makes a face. "I wasn't thinking this was any kind of a news story," she says. "I just thought you might like to see the picture."

"And I did like to see the picture," I say. I should say something more, but I'm not sure what. "We just need to ask so that we don't print anything that people don't want printed."

"Oh, I see," she says. "Well, I guess you can print whatever you like."

Mom likes to watch a television show called *Antiques Road Show*. The point of the show is that most people don't have any idea of the value of the old things they own, so they need help from experts. This holds true for news value as well. Most people are not good judges of the news value of the things in their lives.

As I'm waving Good Bye, I say "You heard me on the radio?"

"I thought you did a very good job."

"Thanks."

She pauses. "I hope you won't give up the paper now that you're on the radio."

"No," I say. "It was just a one-time thing."

"Did you get to meet Brad Pincher?"

"No," I say. "I just talked to him on the phone."

"Well, I thought you did a very good job."

"Thanks."

I never thought much about how Mrs. Everett spends her days, but I wouldn't have guessed it included listening to a guy get worked up about threats to her gun rights. She's so nice, it's hard to imagine her getting worked up herself. I try not to think about her getting washed away in the reservoir flood.

I walk up past the ship-in-a-bottle Bumgarner Ark and press the doorbell. Mrs. Bumgarner opens the door halfway and gives me an x-ray stare. "Yes?"

I try to keep my mind clear and maintain eye contact. Just look at Mrs. Bumgarner and don't think about kissing her daughter's friends while she and Mr. Bumgarner were off buying groceries.

"New edition of the paper. Big story about hunting protests. There's a card inside. Because we're asking everybody to tell us what they think. That's why the card is there."

I keep my eyes glued on Mrs. Bumgarner's eyes and hope that my little spiel didn't give anything away.

"Fifty cents?" she says.

"Yes."

She pays me and I pull out a paper. Before I hand it over, I show her the stuffer card. "Please let us know what you think about the protests. We're going to include people's responses in our next edition."

"I'll take a look," says Mrs. Bumgarner, taking the card and the paper without looking at them and shutting the door.

As I head over to the Fandells, I'm thinking that it was OK that Mrs. Bumgarner answered the door. I probably would have been more awkward with Trish.

When I ring the Fandell doorbell, Jeff opens the door. He's in high school and is a friend of Kyle Butler. He may have been at the meeting at the Butlers' house, but I'm not sure. I think he was there, but it's possible that I just assumed he was there because there were a bunch of people I associate with him.

"New edition of the paper," I say. "Big story about hunting protests. We're asking everybody to call or email and tell us what you think. There's a card inside."

"Good call," he says. "How does this work? Do we pay you something now?"

"Actually, yes, if you have it. This one plus the last one I dropped off makes one dollar."

He disappears. I wonder what he meant by 'Good call.' Good that we're covering the protest? Good that we're asking people's opinions?

Jeff comes back and hands me a dollar. I hand him the paper. "You must know all about this stuff. You're a friend of Kyle's, right?"

"Yeah," he says. "Kyle is a great guy and super smart, but that Deerwalking stuff is messed up."

This seems pretty catchy to me. I pull out my pod. "Can we quote you on that?"

Jeff looks very uncomfortable. "I don't know," he says. "Man, I don't know. That stuff is messed up but Kyle is my friend."

I'm holding the pod and waiting.

Jeff says, "I need to think about this. I got no quote now."

"Sure," I say. "There's a card in the paper with our numbers and stuff. If you want to give us a quote, just give a call or send us a message."

As I head up to the next house, the Luebkers, I'm thinking that was interesting. Jeff is in high school and isn't a dork and he was uncomfortable because he didn't know what he wanted to say to me. That's the power of the pen. I'm sorry he was uncomfortable, but I like feeling like I have a little power. I'm on the radio and high school kids are careful about what they say to me. I'm hoping that doesn't make me a bad person.

Mrs. Luebker is on my list of people with missing pets notices this year. I ring the bell and there she is.

"Hi! New edition of the paper. Big story about hunting protests. There's a card inside for your feedback."

She gives me a brave smile. Mr. Luebker is the manager of a local minor league baseball team. Last summer he moved to Hartford to live with his reportedly hot girlfriend, leaving Mrs. Luebker to mow their lawn and buy newspapers from me. She hands me a dollar and I give her a paper and change.

"One other thing," I say. "We're doing a follow-up on all the people who posted missing pets notices this year. You posted a notice last May."

"Yes. Yes I did. I guess it was May." She isn't smiling or looking at me anymore.

"I'm sorry if this is unhappy to talk about, but for our follow up we're wondering if you ever got your cat back."

She looks around and then looks at me and then looks around some more. "No. I didn't get the cat back. But I did - I did find out where it was. I guess you might call it a kind of a misunderstanding."

Maybe there's a limit to how much a journalist I am, because I don't want to know any more. "OK," I say. "Thank you. That's very helpful. Have a good day."

The other response I get to the follow-up comes later on my route. When I get back around to the Olsons at 35 Springbrook, I ask Mrs. Olson about Pepper. The Olsons put a missing pet notice for Pepper in the Tribune back in the summer.

Mrs. Olson flinches when I ask the question. "No," she says. "We never heard anything. Never got any leads."

"What happened?" I ask.

"She slept outside in the summer. We have a fenced back yard with a doghouse. One morning she was just gone."

"Oh." I make a note in my pad. "Sorry to bring it up. Congratulations on your new puppy."

Heading back from the end of Springbrook, I consider what might have happened to Pepper.

What?

I look right but there's nothing there. I feel something fluttering through the bag on my left hip. I spin around. Cuth Drummond is standing there with one of my papers. I just fell for a really stupid old trick. He must have reached around to tap me on the right shoulder while he stole it.

"Hey!" I say.

Cuth is a fourth grader, which means in theory that he shouldn't be messing with me. Social pecking order starts with grade level. The coolest, most popular fourth grader ranks below the uncoolest, least popular fifth grader. The coolest fifth grader ranks below the uncoolest sixth grader. Cuth is two full rungs down from me and shouldn't even look me in the eyes. These things are enforced by the group in the school yard or the bus stop, but there's no group here now.

"Give it back!" I say. It seems like the obvious and necessary thing to say, but I don't like the way it sounds. It sounds whiny, and I know immediately that Cuth isn't going to give the paper back.

"Sure!" he says with a smile and holds it out to me. When I reach for it, he jerks it away and backpedals. "Oops!"

Cuth has two tough-guy older brothers. Being a bully is sort of the family business. Still, this is pretty humiliating for me already. Sixth graders aren't supposed to get bullied by fourth graders.

I take a step towards him. "Give it back, stupid!" Again, even as I say it, I feel it as a tactical mistake. 'Stupid' isn't nearly strong enough to give me any street cred. Cuth just laughs.

Cuth is kind of a weird name. I think maybe it's short for Cuthbert. His brothers are Uther and Bert. Maybe they call him Cuth instead of Cuthbert so that he doesn't get confused with Bert.

"Come get it," he says. It's a taunt, a dare. Cuth is a fast runner and, while he's a little smaller than I am, he isn't much smaller and he's almost certainly more practiced at fighting than I am. I do some horse-around wrestling with Brian and that's about it. Also, I'm wearing a sport coat and have a bag of papers over my shoulder.

"Jerk face!" I say. This is a little better than 'stupid' but doesn't really change the situation.

Cuth makes a face. "Oh, are you mad because I took one of your [stupid] papers?" he says. Then does a little hop step forward and gives me a kick in shins.

The kick doesn't really hurt but it kills me. My brain freezes up. My stupid eyes water. I'm helpless.

"You know what?" says Cuth. "I don't want your [stupid] paper. It's all a bunch of [garbage]!" And he tears the paper in half, drops both halves and jogs off down the street. I stand watching him jog further and further away.

Here's how much of a wimp I am. It isn't just the fact that a younger kid – a fourth grader – is able to bully me that hurts so much. It's the fact that anyone wants to be mean to me. Why would anyone want to kick me? You'd think I would be prepared for this, but clearly I'm not.

Cuth is pretty far away now and still jogging, almost skipping.

I'm the biggest loser ever anywhere. I walk around thinking I'm so smart because I play word games with my family, but it's just a house of cards. One puff of air and I collapse, revealed as a spineless moron. Cuth the punk fourth grader isn't just faster and stronger and braver than I am, but is also smarter and sees things more clearly. Me and my [stupid] papers are all a bunch of [garbage].

He's still skipping along as he finally disappears from sight. His disappearance somehow allows me to stir. I look around. There are no cameras or gawking people. It might almost be better if there were cameras and gawking people, because then I would have hit bottom. Now I feel like I'm still falling. I've been utterly humiliated and eventually – because news wants to be told – everyone will know that I've been utterly humiliated, but so far only Cuth and I know.

I take a few steps, pick up the two halves of the torn paper and stuff them into my pocket. Maybe I'm hiding the evidence, but maybe I'm just being neat.

The phrase 'hothouse flower' comes into my head. I'm a hothouse flower. I do fine in the artificial world of the Overthinking Department, but I can't survive an hour on my own in the real world. And somehow what proves the point is the fact that I even know what a hothouse flower is. It takes one to know one.

I have just a few houses left. I'm a little shaky when I give my pitch to Mrs. Jarvis, but she doesn't seem to notice. By the time I get home, I'm acting pretty normal for me, even though I still feel doomed and pathetic.

"We have got to get him back!" says Other Darren. He's talking about Mr. Johnson destroying my football. I'm not brave enough to tell Other Darren about my run-in with Cuth Drummond.

"No we don't," I say. "He's just a mean old man."

"He needs to learn a lesson. We can't let him get away with this. He'll just keep picking on other kids. I have an idea."

"What? What's your idea?"

We go to his garage. He finds a box of sports equipment and pulls out a beat-up football. "I don't need this lousy, old football anymore," he says. "I'm going to donate it to the cause. This is going to be the bait!"

He holds it up and looks at me. I don't get it.

"We're going to doctor it first," he says. "Then we'll throw it into his yard. Wait here just a minute."

He tosses me the football and I stand there fiddling with it while I'm waiting for Other Darren to come back and show me what he means. It's a pretty sad-looking old football. It has a New England logo and an embossed signature of Tom Brady. This rings a bell in my head. Didn't he get in trouble for doing something to a football?

Other Darren comes back with something in his hand. It's a needle like a doctor would use to give you a shot. "Pepper's got diabetes," he says. "Mom gives him a shot every day. Every so often, she switches over to a fresh new needle, so we can use this one and Pepper can still get his shot tomorrow."

"Be careful with that," I say. I hate shots. I hate needles. I'm as confused as ever. I thought 'doctoring' the football was just an expression. Maybe not. Maybe we're going to give it some kind of medicine.

"OK, so here's what I'm thinking," he says. "I'm going to take this needle and dip into that gas can over there and suck up just a little bit of gas and inject it into the football. Not a lot. Just a little, little bit. This football is going to be like the cylinder in a car. A bunch of air and a little bit of gas under pressure. All you need is an ignition source."

"I don't know," I say.

"It's perfect. If he's mean enough to throw this into his stove, he deserves to get scared a little."

Other Darren does the honors with the needle. He injects the gas through the little round rubber thing that you'd use to insert an inflation needle . He looks very smooth doing it. Maybe someday he'll be Doctor Other Darren.

We go to my backyard and he hands me back the football. It doesn't look any different. It doesn't feel any different. I don't even smell gas on it. It's the bait. I give it a soft, diagonal pass into Mr. Johnson's yard.

Before I go to bed that night, I walk down the hall to Brian's room. I can hear the far-away sound of his unamplified guitar.

"Hey," he says. "What's up?"

So I tell him about me and Cuth. I kind of blurt it out, but I don't tell him everything. It's just too embarrassing. Still, I get a little choked up and I think he gets the picture.

He rolls his eyes around, thinking. I like that about him. A lot of people would be in a hurry to say something – either "It's all right!" or "You stupid idiot!"

"Got it. Capeesh," he says. "You know, just for the family honor, I should let Cuth have it. Problem is, Uther would kill me." He sets down his guitar. "You know what Gideon's Quest is?" he asks. I shake my head. "It's an online strategy game. You get a certain amount of space money to spend on a team of robot spaceships. You can buy different powers for each of your spaceships, but everything costs money and you can only spend so much. Then, once you have your team built, you compete against somebody else's team in a kind of capture the flag contest."

"OK," I say.

"Over the years thousands of people have competed against thousands of other people and gotten really good at putting together winning teams. You know what a winning team looks like?"

I shake my head again.

"It's not a bunch of spaceships that try to do everything – that are sort of fast and sort of maneuverable and have pretty good armor and pretty good weapons. Those teams lose. The ones that win have spaceships that are very specialized. They have one that is super, super fast and another one that is super maneuverable and so on. They have crazy spaceships that are lousy at most things but do one weird thing better than any other spaceship anywhere. You following me? We're the spaceships, Darren. God only gets so many dollars to spend on each of us, so none of us is going to be good at everything. Some people – maybe even most people – are fairly good at a lot of things. Those people are pretty lucky, because it's comfortable to be in the world knowing you can do a reasonable job of pretty much whatever you need to do in a given day. Then there are other people where God spent all the money on one crazy thing. It's hard to be one of those people, because you're going to suck at a bunch of things that other people can do fine. But those are the people who push the world forward. Those are the people whose teams win. You think Einstein was a good cook? You think Shakespeare could keep track of time? You think Babe Ruth could write a poem? Actually, I don't know about any of those things, but I'm thinking not. So here's my advice to you, and I'm pretty sure this is going somewhere. My advice is that when you find that you suck at something – say, for example, dealing with obnoxious twerps – don't be down about it. Don't say *'Woe is me - I'm no good at beating up proto-criminals who really deserve to be beat up!'* Instead, take it as a positive. If you suck at that, it means that God didn't waste any money on that feature. The money got saved up for the crazy stuff you can do better than anybody. The more stuff you suck at, the greater the chance that you're some kind of Einstein or Shakespeare."

"Or Babe Ruth," I say. "I'm pretty good at pointing to fences."

Usually, after I brush my teeth I put on my pajamas and head to bed where I read a bit and then turn out my light. Tonight, I find Mom, who's sitting on the couch in the den watching a show and doing some kind of sewing repair on a shirt. She looks up at me and pauses the show.

"How many times this week have you worn that shirt?" she asks me.

This is Classic Mom. I don't know if it's technically a non sequitur if nothing came before it, but it's certainly random. She seems serious, like she expects an answer, but I don't know how anyone could answer a question like that. You'd have to keep a chart of your clothing or have some kind of schedule on the inside of your shirt.

"I don't know," I say.

"Well, you might think about mixing things up a bit."

"Sure." I sit down on the couch. "Just a thought," I say. "Take that little round mirror that's in the bathroom and paint on it – on the mirror surface but around the edges so you can still see it's a mirror. You paint flames and pitchforks. OK? And you go to the party as Hell In Mirror."

She smiles at me.

"It's not perfect," I say. "It ought to be Mirren. But it's a thought anyway."

She laughs and gives me a big hug. "You clever doofus!" she says. "That's a lovely idea, but the party was last night! I went as Uma Thurman with the dice but not wearing a beard or anything. Nobody could figure it out – even after I explained it. Now I know. I should have gone as Hell In Mirror! Oh, well. Of course, I couldn't figure out any of the costumes. Apparently there are new movie stars since your Dad and I had you kids and stopped going to movies that aren't animated. Not that I'd trade you kids for a life of movie-watching. You guys are my movie stars. Now get to bed!"

As I head to bed, I think maybe that should be my new title on the masthead of the paper:
Darren McAlpine – Clever Doofus.

I'm sitting on my bunk in prison. There are thousands of chalk marks on the wall. I have a beard that reaches to my feet. How did I get here? Then I remember. The horrible explosion that leveled the Johnson house. The police hauling me off in handcuffs. The embarrassing testimony at the trial. What was I thinking?

I'm awake early. I don't have to get ready for church for another hour or more. I put on some play clothes and sneak out to the backyard. Setting foot very briefly in the extreme back corner of the Schipke property, I'm able climb into Mr. Johnson's yard. I feel like a spy in enemy territory. I don't see the football. It's not in the area I would have expected. Maybe I'm too late. I look around in a wider circle and see the football on Mr. Johnson's back porch. I come closer, but there's a shape moving. A sliding glass door opens and there stands Mr. Johnson. I think he expects me to run away, but I come closer.

"Looking for something?" he says.

"Don't put that football in your stove."

He walks over to the football and picks it up.

"That fence is supposed to mean something," he says, going back to the slider.

"The football is a trap. It's like a bomb. We put gasoline in it."

He stares at me a long time. He shakes the football and holds it to his nose. "Makes an interesting story," he says. "You can leave the same way you came in."

He closes the slider and disappears, carrying the football away with him. I stay where I am. Maybe he believes me, but it seems like he doesn't. I feel like I should stick around and see what happens. I think about standing behind a tree in case the house explodes. The day is starting to get brighter. Eventually there's a thud, like somebody set off a firecracker at the bottom of a well. A few minutes after that, he comes out the slider and sits down on a metal chair on the back porch.

"Know what that pellet stove cost me?"

"I am so sorry," I say.

"Twelve hundred dollars. On sale."

"I am really, really sorry."

"Big crack down one side. Don't know if it did anything to the flue. You tried to warn me. I'll give you that."

"I felt bad about it," I say. "I was worried something bad might happen."

"You tried to warn me. You know, if this happened to somebody else, I'd think it was pretty funny."

I walk over to him. "I want to make it up to you."

"Good! You got twelve hundred dollars handy?"

"I thought maybe I could help you out with something."

"What can you do?"

"Not much."

He rubs his chin. "I don't need any bombs made just now."

"I can copy edit," I say.

"You can what?"

"I can copy edit. If you're writing something and you want it to be just so, I can go through and make all the spelling and grammar correct."

He stands up and walks back to the slider. He pulls it open and looks back at me. "Don't go into strange people's houses, but you can make an exception just this once."

The room through the slider is a den. There's a desk with a computer looking back through a window. I guess Mr. Johnson was sitting at his computer when he saw me walking towards the house. It looks like he was reading or writing an email.

"I have a daughter who got very smart in college and married a banker. I would rather she married a bank robber than a banker, but what are you going to do? She sends me these emails and I want to respond but I don't want to embarrass her."

"I can do this," I say. "I can't fix your stove, but I can help you with your emails. What time is it?" There's a clock on the wall. It's getting late. "I have to go get ready for church. Here's what I'm thinking. Don't send the send email yet. Print out what you have so far. I'll go over it and come back later. Maybe sometime this afternoon. All right?"

He nods, then sits down and prints off some pages. He walks over to his printer, picks up the pages and hands them to me. "We'll give it a try,"' he says. "And here – probably easier for you to leave by the front door."

Brian and I come up the aisle, side by side, suited up for service in red robes with white cottas. I suppose it should be embarrassing to appear in public in a dress and a blouse holding some crazy, old-fashioned fire stick, but I'm not embarrassed. Brian and I are a team. We live in the modern world but can still participate in old traditions. Also, the people at church are really nice and the place is kind of an alternate reality. I'll admit, though, that I'd be embarrassed to process up the aisle of my school cafeteria in this get-up, even with Brian.

Just past the communion rail, we stop and bow. We do pretty much everything in a kind of mirror unison. That's how we acolytes roll. The altar is like a big, solid table with a heavy tablecloth hanging down to the floor. There are eight candles on it - four on each side. We step up to the front of the altar to start lighting the candles on our own side. We start from the middle and work outwards, because it's symbolic of God's love reaching out to the world. I'll try not to think about the symbolism when we reverse the process at the end of the service and God's love is apparently being recalled.

As I reach up to light the first candle on my side, I notice that all the candles today are brand-new. They're taller than usual and have never been lit before. I grab my whatsit – I'll call it a lighter even though that seems like an understatement – and hold it as high over my head as I can. The first candle is lit. Brian's height gives him a better angle than me, so his first candle was lit before mine and he pauses just a moment to keep us synchronized. We light our second candles and then our third.

Now I'm looking up at the outer candle on my side, which is maybe a foot taller than the inner candles. This is going to be a reach.

The lighter has a long wick tucked inside a brass tube with a wooden handle. It has a little lever I can use to shorten or lengthen the wick, which makes the flame smaller or larger. I eyeball the height of the candle and shove the wick a good foot and half past the end of the brass tube. Then I grab the lighter at the very bottom and hold it as high as I can and gently wave the lighter back and forth.

I can't see very well what's happening up above, but the idea is to create a dangling fireball just over the top of the candle. I do my gentle shimmy and try to think the flame onto the candle. Meanwhile, the question I'm pondering is: what kind of mistake is this? Is it a mistake in geometry? Is it a mistake in church behavior?

Also, how will I know if and when it's lit? Maybe it's lit already.

I lower my arms, pull back the wick and take a few steps back away to get a better angle. The candle isn't lit.

I step back forward, push the wick back out, reach back up and let my arms sway gently in the breeze. This has got to work eventually.

My arms get tired, and I bring them down again. I shorten the wick again and take a few steps away. Brian comes over to my side. I think he's going to light the candle, but instead he leans over to speak in my ear.

"Earth to Dalrymple," he whispers. "The candle is lit. Let's get going."

I nod, shove down the tab to douse my flame and join Brian back near the altar rail, where we bow in unison. As we turn to process back down the aisle, I catch a glimpse of Mom looking daggers at me. Is she mad because I had trouble getting the candle lit? Then it hits me. She's mad because I'm grinning like an idiot. The message she is sending me is: *"This is church, buster! Wipe that smirk off your face!"*

So this is the deep question of the day for me to ponder. Are there other things I'm struggling to do that I don't realize are done already? How many candles are already lit up there that I'm just too short to see?

I'm back in Mr. Johnson's den. "There's an issue I have to talk to you about," I say.

"OK."

"I don't know if anybody's ever talked to you about this before, but you have a problem with unclear antecedents."

He looks at me like he's wondering if I'm making fun of him.

"What I mean is, you refer to things without explaining what they are. So, if I said to you: *'I'm going to that place with him'* – you wouldn't know what I meant. What place? Who's him?"

I can't tell what he's thinking.

"Here's your email. The blue circles are all places where the antecedent is unclear – at least to me."

He looks at the paper. There are a lot of blue circles.

"Let's look at the first one, OK? *'I don't like either one.'* Either one of what?"

He looks at the paper for a while. "It's those shows she was talking about. They're terrible."

"OK, the first thing to do is to make it clearer. Something like: *I don't like either one of those shows.* OK? Let's just stop and you can make that one clearer."

I wait while he types.

"Now this is something a little different, but while we're here I'd like to make a suggestion. This sentence is not a very friendly way to start off an email to your daughter. See this arrow down here? I'm suggesting you move that bit about hoping she's healthy up to the top. In fact, you might want to add a Hi or Hello in front of that."

I'm bent over a puzzle on my floor when I hear the dinner call. I stand up and feel dizzy. Am I going to fall over? Am I seeing spots? Is this what dunk people feel like? I'm tempted to get back down on the floor, but that doesn't seem right. I don't want to spend the rest of my life sitting on my floor.

I hold my ground and wait. The moment passes. I'm not going to fall over. Everything's back to normal, only maybe there's a little drum pounding in my ear. I'm not sure what just happened. Can an eleven-year-old kid get a heart attack?

Beth has been quiet and mopey, so it falls to Brian to complain about how slow I am to arrive at the table for Sunday dinner.

"A snail! A sloth! A glacier! Slow! Slow! Slow!" he says. "We're starving here!"

"Sorry," I say as I take my place, last again. "I was attacked by a group of terrorists and had to beat them all up before I could make it to the table."

"They were in the bathroom, right?"

"Hey – I don't tell the terrorists where to hang out. I just fight 'em where I find 'em."

"Well, it's your turn to say Grace."

I look around, then say our grace.

"Biksemad!" announces Mom. "Danish hash! One pot dinner tonight, although we've got salad in the bowl as well. One pot and one bowl. That's bik-semad - not bisk-emad." She looks over at Beth. They sometimes do a routine where Mom coaches Beth on how to say the name, while Beth stubbornly continues to say 'biskemad'. Beth isn't playing that game tonight.

"Biscuit mod?" says Dad.

"Sure," says Brian. "It's like a biscuit only it's – you know – mod."

Mom looks over at Beth, who does not look engaged. "Your father and I were the toast of greater Canton high society Friday night. We were Chico Marx and Uma Thurman."

"It doesn't get any cooler than that," says Dad. "In fact, Chico Marx and Uma Thurman were there – dressed up as us."

"Any good costumes this year?" asks Brian, who then adds, "Any other good costumes?"

Dad scrunches up his face. "It wasn't a vintage year for the Deever party."

"I don't know," says Mom. "Bob Harwood is always pretty reliable. He had a tray with some kind of a ginger cookie shaped like the number one and that was it. By way of a hint, he told us the cookie was German."

Brian and I make a bunch of thinking and stalling noises, but eventually we give up.

Mom points to Dad, who smiles and says "Crisp Ein."

We groan.

Mom turns to Beth. "*Ein* is one in German. Crisp Ein is a play on an actor whose name is Chris Pine. He was the voice of the guy from *The Lego Movie*"

Beth shrugs.

"No," I say. "That was Chris Pratt."

"Crisp Rat!" shouts Brian. "Mr. Harwood should have baked a cookie in the shape of a rat!"

Dad hits his forehead. "Oh man! I could have been Crisp Rat!"

Mom holds out her hands. "We could have been Crisp Rat and Hell in Mirror! Oh, well." She looks over at my brother. "So – Brian. What do you have to report?"

"Ho-ho! I won the World History Challenge this week."

"Cool!" says Dad. "How'd you do it?"

"You have to stand behind a line and toss a spider-ball so that it hits the window but then stays on the windowsill. It's wicked hard because the windowsill is only about this wide and usually when you throw the spider-ball hard enough to hit the window it bounces way off and doesn't even think about staying on the windowsill. In order to win the challenge, you have to do it with both the red ball and the blue ball, one after the other."

Dad gives him a high five. "Our son, the world history expert!"

Mom frowns. "I'm sorry. Am I missing something here? What in the world does this have to do with world history?"

"We do this in Mr. Janick's world history class for the last five minutes if we've finished all our work."

"Oh, I see," says Mom. "Apparently, there hasn't been enough world history to keep your class busy for a whole hour."

"I don't know," says Brian. "It gets the kids to finish their work. Also, in English this week we did dramatic readings of scenes from *Romeo and Juliet* – and I got the best part."

There's a pause.

"Romeo?" says Beth.

"Juliet?" I say.

"Tybalt?" says Dad, who knows stuff like this. "Mercutio?"

"I got to do the sound effects. Sword fight!" And – using just his mouth – he crashes and clangs and zips and groans. "Climb up the balcony!" And he creaks and groans and pants and then produces a long, comical kissing sound.

Dad holds out his arms. "World history expert and Shakespearean actor."

Mom turns to me. "And what about you, Darren?"

Brian answers for me. "Props to Darren for being a radio star this week!"

There's a smattering of applause.

"Thanks," I say. "Do you know who's apparently a Brad Pincher listener and heard me on the radio?" I give it a moment. "Mrs. Everett!"

"That's great!" says Dad. "You're famous now in Mrs. Everett's house."

I hold up my fork. "Today Mrs. Everett, tomorrow the world!"

"And Beth?" says Mom, looking at my sister. "What do you have to report?"

Beth looks at her plate. "I don't want to go to school next week."

"Is this about the shoes?"

Beth nods.

"I think your brothers have something they want to say to you." Mom gives us a look.

Brian stands up. "Sorry about giving you a hard time about the shoes."

"Yeah," I say, standing up.

"There's something we want to show you," says Brian. "OK?"

Beth nods OK.

"We'll be right back," I say.

Brian and I beat feet to our respective rooms, put on the clunky, black, ersatz doctor shoes we got and then return together to the table.

"You see these?" says Brian. "If you're going to wear healthy, sensible shoes for a while, then we're going to wear healthy, sensible shoes, too."

"Yeah," I say.

Beth looks at us, but she doesn't say anything.

Mom and Dad stand up. Mom holds up a finger. "We'll be right back!"

I'm not sure what this part is about. Brian and Beth and I stare at one another. After a minute, Mom and Dad walk back in, wearing their own clunky, black, ersatz doctor shoes. We make a huddle connecting back to Beth. She stands up and holds her arms out and joins the huddle crying.

In some ways, my world is getting bigger. I'm learning new things. I can stay up a little later at night. In other ways, though, my world is getting smaller. I'm starting to cross off possibilities in my head. I'm not going to be a professional athlete. I'm not going to participate in an Olympics. To get those places, you need to be at a certain point on your trajectory by the time you hit eleven. I'm not on that trajectory.

In the wake of my fiasco with Cuth Drummond, I've made some more cross-outs. I'm not going to be a soldier or a policeman. I'm not going to be someone who enforces discipline on his own – that is, not a prison guard, not a bus driver, not a teacher. To be honest, I never really saw myself as a prison guard. Until now, though, I had thought teacher would have been a possibility for me.

I'm not saying my life is over. I could still be a movie star. I could still be President of the United States.

We got a pretty good response to our request for comments from our readers. I've edited the best quotes and arranged them into categories for an article.

READERS SHARE THEIR OPINIONS

Thank you to all our readers who shared thoughts about the planned protests against deer hunting. We don't have room to print everyone's response, but here are some sample responses we received. We've arranged them into three categories.

Category 1 - Supporting the Deer Hunters

Plenty of more important problems in the world that kids should be protesting. Deer get shot. Welcome to our world.

Some people hunt deer to feed their families. Get out of the way!

Would you rather be a chicken and be shut up all your life? Better to be a deer and run free while you can.

It's more cruel to let the deer overpopulate and starve.

We're all going to die someday. A bullet while you're out in the woods isn't a bad way to go.

People who hate guns should move to Sweden.

Who cares about deer? If you want to be a human shield, go hang out with young people in the tough sections of Hartford.

Q: What do you call people who dress up like deer during hunting season? A: Menison!

Category 2 - Supporting the Protesters

I'm with the kids on this one. Hunting is dangerous and cruel.

Anyone near the woods might as well be a Deerwalker. A woman in Maine was shot hanging up laundry in her own backyard during hunting season. Nobody went to jail.

We shoot too many kids in this country. The police shoot kids who play with toy guns. How about this for an idea? Let's not shoot any more kids. Period. If that means no deer hunting, then no deer hunting.

Let's arm the deer with their own rifles and see how many hunters want to take their chances with a fair fight. (I believe our Constitution gives us the right to arm bears.)

Category 3 - Concerned About the Safety of the Protesters

I don't know if deer hunting is good or bad. I do know that young people shouldn't be encouraged or even allowed to put their own lives at risk.

God bless the kids who care about the animals, but don't let them go where they might get shot at. Lock them up if necessary!

While I'm at it, I take a shot at the Joint Statement Brian suggested.

JOINT STATEMENT ON DEERWALKING

Does widespread gun ownership and gun use make society safer or less safe? We the undersigned agree on the importance of this question, but we do not agree on the answer. We disagree on most issues regarding guns. Today, however, we speak with one voice regarding a gun-related issue on which we do agree.

Some of our fellow citizens oppose the shooting of animals. They have every right to hold and express such opinions.

However, we oppose protests that interfere with legal sport hunting. We particularly oppose the form of protest known as "Deerwalking" in which protesters attempt to use themselves as human shields for the hunted animals. This practice creates an unacceptable physical risk to the protesters and an unacceptable emotional risk to the hunters.

We look forward to discussing these issues with one another, with the hunting protesters and with the community at large. We strongly believe that these issues should be decided through discussions and elections - and not from either the sending or the receiving end of a gun.

Brad Pincher

The Brad
Pincher Show

Theodore Cernak

Repeal2ndAmendment.org

Dad has a drink in his hand and is wearing an old-fashioned hat. He looks like something out of a black-and-white movie. "Welcome to the Overthinking Department," he says, "where overthinking isn't just a way of life, it's more. It's more than a way or maybe it's a way of more than a life. Or, alternately, it's a way of life that is more. It's at least one of those things, and maybe, you know – what's the word?"

"More!" Brian and I shout.

"So what do we have?" asks Dad.

"We have a bunch of reader responses," I say. "I picked some I thought might be worth publishing and organized them into three categories." I hold up my draft. "Also, I have two possible stories from Mrs. Everett."

"Question about an ad," says Brian.

"I've got nothing useful," says Dad. "I'm looking for a mnemonic."

"I'll bite," says Brian. "What do you need?"

"A mnemonic. Some trick to remember something. The thing I want to remember is counting centuries. For some reason, I've been in conversations or watching shows lately where they're talking about the Fourteenth Century or the Nineteenth Century or the Tenth Century. And I have to stop and think about what that means. I know you add one or subtract one. I know the Fourteenth Century means either the thirteen hundreds or the fifteen hundreds. But which one is it? It takes me a while to work it out, and I miss stuff. It's like I know the time in Chicago is an hour ahead or an hour behind. I need a good, fast way to remember how this works so that I can learn some history before I become a historical relic myself."

We pause and think. "I got nothing," I say. "What's the answer? Do you add or subtract?"

Brian says, "Subtract. The nineteen hundreds were the Twentieth Century. This is the Twenty-first Century. So the Fourteenth Century had to be the thirteen hundreds. You also subtract if you want to know the time in Chicago. Maybe that's how you can remember."

Dad looks at Brian. "How do you remember?"

"Bam! The Twentieth Century was the nineteen hundreds. That's how I remember. I don't know why I don't use my own century. Maybe the term gets used more because the Twentieth Century is over. You say 'The Twenty-First Century' and it doesn't mean much to me at this point."

"Yeah," I say. "It sounds like a real estate sign."

"Still looking for a mnemonic," says Dad.

"Century comes before Hundreds alphabetically," I say. "So Hundreds, coming later, gets to be more. Thirteenth Century – Fourteen Hundreds."

"Or you could think about the beginning," says Brian. "Year one up to year ninety-nine. That's the First Century, right? But it's the no-hundreds."

You could write it on your hand," I say.

"Make a chart," says Brian. "Year numbers and century numbers lined up. Tape it to the mirror in your bathroom."

"Some kind of a catchy little song or rhyme," I say. I point at my brother. "Brian will write it for you."

"Sure," he says, pointing back at me. "Darren will write the lyrics and I'll write the music."

"Done!" says Dad. "I'm looking forward to it."

I look at Brian. "What rhymes with 'century'?"

He shrugs. "Benchury. Kenchury. Denchury. 'Your teeth are looking very dentury today!'"

"OK," says Dad, turning to Brian. "What's the question about the ad?"

He pulls out a piece of paper. "Mr. DeBisschop wants to buy an ad. Here's the text he gave me." He picks up the paper and reads:

> *Think Twice Before You Loan Power Tools or Anything Else to Bruce Onstott of 15 Glenbrook Circle. You Might Not Get Them Back or They Might Be Broken. This Is What Happened To Me –Two Good Electric Sanders Ruined!*
>
> *Horace DeBisschop, 17 Glenbrook Circle*

Dad listens without responding. He looks at me. "Darren?"

"That ad might be the best thing in our next paper!" I say. "Is it real? Is there a Bruce Whatsisname on Glenbrook Circle?"

"Absolootle," says Brian. "He's a real person and he buys a paper sometimes. I don't know if Mr. DeBisschop is really p-o'ed at him or if it's some kind of a joke between them."

"I think it's hysterical," I say.

He looks at Dad. "Can you see why I'm worried about it, though? He's talking a little smack here. Is there a line we need to worry about? Can I take out an ad to say Darren's ugly and his Momma dresses him funny?"

"Hey!"

"Sure, I see why you're worried about it," he says. Then, to us both: "What could go wrong?"

Brian and I look at each other. "Mr. Whatsisname could go ballistic," I say. "He could sue Mr. DeBisschop and sue us and take us all hostage."

Brian looks at me like he's giving me a hint. "And what would happen after he took us hostage?" he asks.

I think about it. "We'd probably get returned eventually," I say. "But we might not work anymore."

This seems to be the answer he was looking for and we high five.

Dad presses on. "And what could we do to minimize the risk?"

Again, Brian and I look at each other.

"Treat it like a political ad," he says. "Label it as a paid advertisement."

"Maybe we should talk to Whatsisname," I say. "Give him a chance to tell his side of the story."

"I like that," says Dad. "It's better than making him buy his own ad. Should we tell him what's in the ad before we run it?"

Brian rubs his nose. "Maybe. We should ask Mr. DeBisschop if it's OK for us to read the ad to the other guy. If he says No, then we ask him afterwards. If he says Yes, then we ask him ahead of time."

Dad turns to me. "Does that sound good to you?" he asks.

"Sure," I say.

"OK," he says. "Brian – you're going to check back with Mr. DeBisschop?"

"Yeah," he says.

"OK. Darren – what have you got for us?"

I hand over the paper with the quotes. Dad and Brian skootch together to read it at the same time. I try to zone out. In my daydream, there's a knock at the door. I answer it and Lucille is standing on the porch. "You're too old for me," I say. She sighs and steps aside. Mrs. DiFuria is standing behind her, looking stricken.

"Good work," says Dad. "These look almost too good. How much did you edit them?"

"A bit," I say. "The written ones were the worst. Grown-ups cannot spell. Kids have to take all these spelling tests and meanwhile grown-ups can't spell the simplest words. I also put some of the quotes on a little bit of a diet. But they're all just polished up versions of real quotes. I didn't make any of them up."

"Which one makes me nervous?" he asks.

"Menison," I say.

"It's a wise son who knows his father," he says.

"It's just a joke," says Brian. "We can use a few jokes."

"Kind of a creepy joke," says Dad.

We sit for a moment, staring at the paper. Even I am staring at the paper, although I can't read it from where I am. Dad looks up at me.

"What do you think, Darren?" he says.

"These are the opinions in the neighborhood - edited down and with the spelling fixed. If this one is kind of creepy, then that's part of the picture."

"Plus, it's a joke," says Brian.

"Plus we're trying to stir up some media coverage," I say.

"My vote would still be No," says Dad. "I'm happy for us to give a forum to a broad range of opinions, but I wouldn't for example want to print some kind of hate speech. But I'm not invoking my executive veto on this one. We'll see what other opinions come in, but if both of you want to include this quote in the article, you can do it. Do we have anything else on the Deerwalking story?"

"We have some Brad Pincher quotes and Brian talked to a local guy from the Repeal the Second Amendment group. There's probably a story we could get out of playing them off one another.

Brian suggested we get them to agree to a Joint Statement. Probably a long shot, but here's a draft."

I hand over the paper with the Joint Statement and zone out while they read it.

"Interesting," says Dad. "Do we want them to play nice with each other?"

"This could make news," says Brian. "This is infrared and ultraviolet."

"OK. But it does sound like a longshot. What else do we have on this story?"

I shrug. "We could update one of the editorials we didn't use last time."

"It's feeling too passive to me," says Dad. "The newspaper business isn't about sitting around waiting for something to happen so you can write it down. Sometimes you've got to squeeze the news out – like squeezing out a zit!"

"There's an image," says Brian.

"Suggestions?"

Brian and I look at each other.

"Kyle," I say. "We should interview Kyle."

"Now you're talking!" says Dad. "Invisible Kyle is sitting in that chair. What do we ask him?"

"Where did this come from?" I say. "Why deer hunting?"

"Where did you get the idea for Deerwalking?" says Brian.

"How did you get so invisible?" I say.

"What do you say to people who don't like Deerwalking?" says Brian. "Not because they like deer hunting, but because they disagree with the tactic. What do you say to people who say that this kind of protest is going to get people killed?"

"What do you think could go wrong?" I say. "What do you worry about?"

"Are there any alternative forms of protest that you'd consider?" says Brian.

"I'm eleven years old," I say. "Would you want me to come along as a Deerwalker?"

We sit quietly for a bit. "I like it," says Dad. "Who's going to do the interview?"

"Darren," says Brian.

"You're closer to Kyle's age," I say.

"Exactly," he says. "That last one works better coming from you. It would work even better coming from Beth, but I'll settle for you."

"Works for me," says Dad. "Now, what's up with Mrs. Everett?"

"I haven't written anything up," I say, "but I took a couple of photos last Saturday." I pull out my pod and open the camera roll. "I don't know if you remember her old dog, Punkin. This is a picture Mrs. Everett has of her granddaughter with a new dog her family got that she says looks just like Punkin and they call the dog Punkin Two. This is a huge metal statue of Abraham Lincoln created by Mrs. Everett's son that sits on the couch in Mrs. Everett's living room. The statue sits on the couch. When you turn a switch, its hat lights up. Should I write up one or both of those items as a story? And - if only one - which one?"

"I remember Punkin," says Dad.

"Sure," says Brian. "Mrs. Everett had Punkin forever. She loved that old dog."

"I was sort of surprised she didn't get Punkin Two herself," says Dad. "I guess maybe she feels like she's too old now to take care of a dog, especially maybe a young dog."

"Whoa! That Lincoln thing is crazy," says Brian. "It must take up half her living room."

"It's huge," I say.

"What kind of dog was Punkin?" asks Dad.

"It think it was a beagle," I say.

"What's the question again?" asks Brian.

"I don't see how I can combine these two stories. And I'm not crazy about having two articles about Mrs. Everett in one issue. It's going to look like we're playing favorites. So which one do we use first?"

We look at Dad, who looks at my brother. "Brian?" he says.

"The statue is crazy, but Punkin was part of the neighborhood. Gotta go with the dog."

I look at Dad.

"I'd recommend writing up both stories if you can. Sometimes it becomes obvious what's the stronger story once you write it up. But I expect Brian is right. I don't think even Abraham Lincoln can compete against the second coming of Punkin."

This isn't the answer I was expecting. I thought for sure that the unbelievable statue was a killer story and that a dog that resembles another, deceased dog was a non-story. They're the same breed – of course they look alike!

But I guess I was wrong. Apparently still a few things left for me to learn.

4. Superman Has a Lot of Reasons for Not Getting Into Fights

Brian doesn't go trick or treating any more. One more disadvantage of getting older. I still go and am saved from being embarrassed about it by the fact that I'm needed to escort my little sister. Beth always goes as a princess. She has the whole princess thing down to a science, including glitter make-up and a wand that lights up at the end. Out on our rounds, the wand functions as an almost-flashlight, and she has a button-hole in her sash that she can use to holster her wand when she needs two hands.

I never know what to go as. I usually make up something pretty specious on the afternoon of the big day. Just the other day, I had an idea for Mom's outfit for the Deever party. It was a day late, but it was an idea, which is what I don't have for my own costume. I blame this on the fact that Halloween doesn't have a theme. I was thinking about Mom's party outfit when I should have been thinking about my Halloween costume because the party theme made it like a puzzle to solve.

So what will I go as? I could be a hobo. That's the scraping-the-barrel option. You'd think the scraping-the-barrel option would be cutting eyeholes in a sheet and going as a ghost, but the visibility is terrible, so it isn't really a viable costume, especially if you're trying to keep an eye on a little sister. Meanwhile, you can always rip up some old clothes and dirty your face and be a hobo. I could be a pirate. We've got an eye-patch somewhere from Brian's appearance as Fagin in a school production of Oliver Twist. Unfortunately, the Fagin in this particular production didn't sport either a parrot or a peg-leg. I'd like to be a cartoon superhero, but you need a good outfit to be a superhero. A red towel around my neck and a felt marker S on a tee shirt isn't going to get the job done. I think about being a neighborhood Deerwalker and going as a deer. Maybe I could rig up some antlers out of tree branches, but probably it wouldn't work. How would I attach them to my head? How would I lean over a bowl of candy?

Have you ever seen the movie *Apollo 13*? There's a scene where they dump a box of stuff onto a table and tell the scientists they have to make some kind of a machine out of the stuff on the table. I decide to take a walk around the house and collect the stuff that I could use to make a Halloween costume. I'll put the stuff in a box and then pour it on a table and tell myself I need to make a costume out of this stuff.

When my sister and I head out on Halloween, mostly I like to stick to the streets that make up Brian's newspaper route. I want the people on my own route to think of me as a young journalist and not a trick-or-treating kid. So now we're heading up to the door of the Patel house. Brian often has a story to tell about Mr. Patel giving him a hard time about the paper. Mr. Patel doesn't complain about the content of the paper. He says we don't have a good business model. It isn't scalable. We can't monetize it. I'm not sure what this means exactly, but I think it boils down to the pretty obvious fact that we aren't going to get rich running our newspaper. Brian says he can't tell if Mr. Patel is being serious or not. He says he seems serious, but how can anyone be serious scolding a couple of neighborhood boys about their business model?

"What a beautiful princess!" says the woman at the door. "A fairy princess with a wand!"

"Thank you," says Beth. "Trick or treat."

The woman turns to me. "And what are you?"

"Ah'm a wun-eyed hobo!" I announce in the Southern drawl that I've decided is the manner of speaking appropriate to a one-eyed hobo. I actually look a bit like Fagin and thought about doing a cockney accent.

The woman makes no further comment, but drops a candy in each of our bags, so I guess the costume was good enough. I don't eat a lot of candy, but I like to know it's there when I want it. A reasonable Halloween haul will keep my candy drawer stocked until the Easter refill.

We're working our way down Cedar Crest. Next up is the Edelstein-Pratt house, which is occupied by two gay men. One is tall and easy-going and the other is short and sarcastic. I don't know which is Edelstein and which is Pratt. It makes me wonder how much our bodies affect our personalities. Would the sarcastic guy be more easy-going if he were taller? Would the easy-going guy be more sarcastic if he were shorter? How would I act if, for example, I were big and muscular?

"Hey McAlpine! Boss patch!"

This is Connor Morillo, who's my age and dressed up as a Red Sox baseball player, including a beard. He and his sister, Dede, have just gotten some Edelstein-Pratt candy and we're passing them on the path to the front door. Dede is Beth's age and they play together sometimes. "Boss" is a word Connor uses for things he likes.

"Thanks," I say. "How's it going?"

"We own the night!"

Connor aims his flashlight up into the sky and waves it around. This actually is a pretty good way to show that you don't own the night. The dark sky swallows up the beam as if it never existed. Beth and Dede say a quiet Hi to each other.

Last year, Beth and Dede had a brief but pretty successful venture selling scented pine cones. They collected the pine cones from the Morillos' back yard and sprayed perfume on them and tied ribbons around them and went around together with a wagon selling them door to door. I think they earned more than the

Tribune that week. The asking price was a quarter, but many people paid more. One woman gave them five dollars.

I wonder sometimes if the Tribune is a scented pine cone. Maybe people buy it because they think it's cute and they want to be nice to the neighborhood kids.

I point up towards the Edelstein-Pratt door. "We're just going to hit this house."

Connor leans closer to me. "Ask him for a UNICEF donation and they'll give you a buck."

Beth and I go to the door, which opens before we have a chance to ring the bell. "Trick or treat!" we say.

It's the tall guy. He tells us how great we look and drops a candy bar in each of our sacks. I don't ask for money.

Connor and Dede haven't moved. "Which way are you guys headed?" asks Connor.

We've been working our way down the hill towards Glenwood." I point.

"We just came from that way," he says. I figure that means we'll split up, but they keep walking with us down the hill to the next house. I think Dede is supposed to be the Star Wars woman. She has a big, Uzi-like squirt gun on her back with a strap over her shoulder.

The next house is dark. "Dark house, you lose!" says Connor. Then he leans over. "I mailed them an egg!"

"That's Mrs. Rousseau," I say. "You can't expect her to hand out candy. She's like a hundred years old."

"Oh." He stops and looks around. "Is she like a friend of yours?"

"Not really. It's the newspaper. I know who lives in pretty much every house in the neighborhood because of the newspaper."

"You're kidding?" He points diagonally across the street. "Who lives there?"

"Pinkertons. Mrs. Pinkerton sometimes buys an ad for the jewelry she makes."

"Over there." He's pointing diagonally the other way.

"Lopez-Mahoney. The man is Lopez and the woman is Mahoney."

"That is so boss! That's like a superpower!"

"This isn't even his route," says Beth.

I point to the Lopez-Mahoney house. "It used to be the Bohanan house," I say. "They moved to Florida." At this point, I'm showing off.

Connor looks back at the dark Rousseau house. "The lady here is a hundred years old? I didn't know. I thought it was just some greedy kid-haters." He walks over to the mailbox, opens it up and shines his flashlight in. "Oh, man!" He shines the flashlight onto the lawn, then hands me his Halloween sack. "Just a second." He walks over and picks up a pine cone which he takes back to the mailbox and uses to wipe the shell and guts of a cracked egg out of its insides.

"Ew!" says Dede.

"Gross!" says Beth.

Connor holds up the drippy pine cone, shines his flashlight at it and looks at Beth and Dede. "Who wants to eat the monkey brains?"

There are no takers. Beth and Dede are used to a more refined class of pine cone. He shrugs, tosses it into some bushes and takes back his sack of candy from me. He leans over to say something in my ear. "This is fun! Maybe sometime us and our sisters we could – you know – double date."

Double date? I thought Connor was wound up on a sugar high, but he's trying to impress Beth. That seems creepy to me. And he thinks I'd be interested in Dede, which also seems creepy.

"This street is dead," he says. "Let's try Deepwood."

"Come back!" It's a shout from the Pinkerton house across the street. "Come back, you stupid dog!"

It's hard to see because it's mostly black, but a medium-sized dog runs down the Pinkerton lawn, across the street and into Mrs. Rousseau's side yard.

"Let's get it!" shouts Connor, and we all take off, following the dog. There's no fence between Mrs. Rousseau's yard and the Greens next door to her, but both yards have fences at the back. There's maybe a foot between the ends of the two fences. Connor and I aim our flashlights at the dog, which disappears through the gap. We all run to the spot. "Watch out!" I yell. "There's a cliff here!"

'Cliff' maybe is an overstatement. A foot or two past the fences, there's a four or five foot drop to the yard below. Connor gets down first and runs on. I stop at the bottom to help Dede down. "Where's Beth?" I ask.

"I don't know," she says, running after Connor.

I climb back up and between the fences. Beth is in the backyard of the Greens. I jog over to her. "I thought I saw something over this way," she says, pointing with her wand.

"I'll go around the other way."

I pass Mrs. Pinkerton, who is heading for the gap between the fences and yelling "Come back you stupid dog!"

When I make it around to the other side of the Greens' yard, I see Beth moving very slowly towards some bushes. "Hey, Max!" she says. "You've had a hard run!" She reaches into her Halloween bag and pulls out a little cardboard box of candies. She sets the bag on the ground and works open the top of the box without letting go of her wand. Then she holds the box in her wand hand and uses her free hand to hold up a disk of candy. "Ooh, Max! Look at this! It might look like medicine, but don't be fooled, Max. This is tasty, tasty! You're going to love it!" The closer she gets to the bush, the lower she gets and the slower she goes. "Hey, Max! Yum! Yum! Yum!" She pretends to lick and chew on the candy, smacking her lips.

She reaches towards the bush and I see a shape, a dog nose, held up, waiting. I think of Adam on the Sistine Chapel, waiting to be touched by the holy finger.

And it's done. The dog has the candy and Beth is holding its collar.

"Well done!" I say. "Here, I can hold the collar."

"I've got it. You can get my bag. Please."

I get her bag.

"And help me get another candy. You want another one, don't you, Max?"

I take the little box from her and hand her a candy, which she gives to the dog. Then we walk across the yard, across the street and up some steps and a concrete walk to the Pinkerton door. I ring the bell. A man – I assume it's Mr. Pinkerton – opens the door.

"Trick or treat!"

"Lady? Is that Lady? Thank you so much! Come here, Lady." He grabs the dog by the collar and yanks it into the house and swats it pretty hard. "Bad dog! Bad dog!" He looks up at us. "I'll be right back." He marches the dog off into the house, muttering angrily at it. We hear a door slam. The man reappears at the door. "Thank you so much for bringing that crazy dog back. I'm not sure how she got out. Here, let me give you some candy."

"No, thank you," says Beth coldly, and she turns and leaves. I give Mr. Pinkerton a quick look and follow her.

"I thought you knew the dog," I say when I catch up with her. "I thought it was Max."

She rolls her eyes. "I know her now." I hand Beth her Halloween bag. She looks back at the Pinkerton house. "Those people are mean," she says. "No wonder Max wanted to run away."

We seem to have lost Connor and Dede. Maybe it's just as well. I don't know if Beth could tell that Connor was trying to impress her, but I bet should could. She's very tuned in to boy-girl stuff. I think about asking her about it, but decide not to. Don't ask the question if you don't really want to know the answer.

Beth and I head back across to the Greens. If I think Connor should leave Beth alone, maybe somebody else would think that Megan Boucher should leave me alone. Maybe they'd be right. Maybe I should start thinking about Becca Hennessey. She's pretty cute now, and it'll be a long time before she looks like her grandma.

Wednesday night, first night of November, I'm reading in bed, *The Two Towers*. Pippin just looked into the palantir, the magical ball, the seeing stone. He shouldn't have done it, but maybe it'll work out. A seeing stone can help you and hurt you at the same time. You get information from it, but it lets your enemies get information from you. It might be a metaphor, but it might not. Tolkien was writing before there was an internet.

Dad looks in on me.

"Hey," he says.

"Hey." I put a marker in my place.

"What's Superman's secret identity?" he says.

"You mean his name when he was a baby on Krypton?"

"No," he says. "His identity day-to-day when he's not saving the world and stuff."

"Clark Kent," I say.

He nods. "Describe Clark Kent to me."

"He's a newspaper reporter. Wears glasses. Mild mannered."

"Mild mannered newspaper reporter," says Dad. "Just what I was fishing for. So here's the deal. Every so often, when Clark Kent is out somewhere not being Superman, he'll have to deal with somebody who's being a real jerk. It's a classic scene in the Superman stories, right? Clark Kent and Lois Lane are in line for a movie and some jerk cuts in front of them and calls Clark Kent a name."

At this point I've caught up to the situation. Brian has talked to Dad about my run-in with Cuth. Dad is here to give me some kind of pep talk.

"What happens in those stories?" he asks.

I think for a moment. "He takes it," I say. "He doesn't let himself get into fights when he's Clark Kent."

"Ah," says Dad. "Why not?"

I sigh. It seems to me that Superman has a lot of reasons for not getting into fights as Clark Kent, but those reasons don't include fear of getting beaten up by a fourth grader.

"I don't know," I say. "For one thing, he doesn't want to give away the fact that he's Superman. Also, it's not like a jerk could hurt him."

"Maybe," says Dad, which is his code word for *'you're wrong'*. "Is Superman a robot?"

"No,"

"Does Superman have feelings?"

"Yes."

"So," says Dad, "A jerk could hurt his feelings, right?"

"Yes. But he can't give away the fact that he's Superman."

"Hold on," he says. "Let me get this straight. When the jerk cuts in line and calls Clark Kent a name and he just shrugs it off and lets the guy stay in front of him in line. You're saying that he would knock that guy into another dimension, only he knows he can't get away with it. That it would blow his cover?"

I nod "Yeah. Sure. Why do you think he just takes it?"

"I think he takes it because it takes focus to be Superman. I don't care how many superpowers you have, it's still a hard job. You have to protect the world against supervillains. You don't have a lot of time or attention to waste on jerks. It's like if you're out on safari hunting for a lion, you don't want to start shooting at rabbits."

When I turn out the light and get ready to sleep, it strikes me that Dad's pep talk worked. It was pretty corny and not totally convincing, but still I feel better. I like the image of Cuth Drummond as a rabbit that isn't worth shooting and I'm glad Dad wants to give me a pep talk after something bad happens to me.

I'm meeting Kyle at his house at four o'clock. I'm staring at the garden two houses up because it's only three fifty-five. I wasn't sure how long it would take me to walk over here.

I'm thinking this is an important year for me. This could well be my peak non-adult year. Next year I become a teenager – and who knows what that's going to be like? Chances are that I'll regress before I start moving forward again. So I need to make the most of this year. Make hay while the sun shines. I'm pretty sure that's the right expression, although I don't understand it. How does anyone make hay?

I get to the front door at four sharp. Kyle answers it.

"Hey," he says.

"Hi," I say.

He lets me in and we sit in the living room. He sits in a big chair and I sit on the sofa. It seems like a mistake somehow to sit on the sofa – too much room around me.

"It's pretty cool," he says. "You and your brother doing the paper."

"Thanks," I say. It seems rude not to compliment him back for something, but I can't think of anything appropriate to say. I pull out my pod. "Would it be OK if I record this?" I ask.

"I guess."

I hit the record button and pull out a little notepad. I wrote out some questions ahead of time, but my handwriting is really bad.

"What first got you interested in the issue of deer hunting?" I say.

Kyle smiles, leans back and talks and talks. He has always loved animals and been interested in nature. He went camping with his uncle's family once and saw people shooting animals for the first time - birds and squirrels. It seemed cruel and wrong to him ("It's their woods, right?") but he liked the people. He didn't think his uncle or his uncle's friends were bad people. As he grew up, he's been involved with various groups working on global warming, and this led him to other environmental issues. Through environmental groups, he got to know some people who work for the state. The state department that oversees hunting is the Department of Environmental Protection and he described a tension in the department between people who are die-hard environment protectors and those who want to run the department like a business. Apparently for the state there's money in deer hunting, and so the people who don't like deer hunting complain about it to their environmental friends.

He describes a website one of his friends pointed out to him and I start getting nervous. We're ten minutes into this interview and I feel like it's gotten away from me. I'm going to have to interrupt him.

"Excuse me," I say.

"Yeah?"

"I think I have enough on how you got started with deer hunting. I'd like to ask you another question."

"Oh," he says. "Sure."

"Where did the idea of Deerwalking come from?"

"I first heard about it through that chat group I mentioned. I heard a report about a hiking club somewhere in Pennsylvania that organized a Deerwalk for opening day of the hunting season a few years back. I don't know if they came up with the idea themselves or borrowed it from somebody else. I was hoping to track down someone from the club, but haven't managed to do it. And I'll stop there so you can ask another question if you want to."

I look at my notepad.

"I'm wondering what you say to people who say that Deerwalking is bad," I say.

"What do I say?"

"Yes."

"To people who say Deerwalking is bad?"

"Yes."

"I guess I'd start with explaining about population control. There are options. Some people think that there aren't any options. You either shoot them or they overpopulate and then wreck the forest or starve. But there are in fact a whole host of other options, starting with birth control. People think that birth control for deer is some kind of joke, like deer are going to use-"

He looks at me and stops. Maybe he was going to use some rude slang or maybe he just doesn't want to talk about sex – even sex between animals – with somebody my age. Meanwhile, I'm glad he stopped.

"Actually," I say. "Actually, I'm wondering what you say to people who might even agree with you about deer hunting but don't agree with Deerwalking as a tactic. Because of, you know, putting people in danger."

"Oh." He thinks for a moment. "Here's an analogy. Say you have a pet dog and some mean people come around and shoot whipped cream at your dog's face as a joke, to make it look like your dog has rabies. And your Mom comes home and sees your dog foaming at the mouth and she, like, freaks out and goes and gets a gun to shoot it. And you're screaming at her, 'Don't shoot it! Don't shoot it!' But she isn't paying any attention to you. So what do you do? You stand in front of the dog is what you do. You stand in front of the dog and wave your arms and shout 'Don't shoot! The dog doesn't have rabies! It's just whipped cream!' You aren't standing there to get shot. You're standing there to make sure the dog doesn't get shot, right?"

There's a part of me that's thinking this is a pretty far-fetched analogy that doesn't quite apply to Deerwalking. There's another part of me that's struggling to think about how I can write up this interview for a 250-word article. There's also a big part of me that's standing in front of Johann and yelling at Mom to put down the gun. I look back at my notes.

"What about me? I'm eleven years old. Would you want me to be a Deerwalker?"

He makes a face. "I don't want anybody to be a Deerwalker. I don't want to be a Deerwalker. I want lots of people to come march to the reservoir on Saturday. But no, I don't think anybody should be a Deerwalker. I just want to be able to say there will be Deerwalkers to discourage the hunters on opening day and get people to think about this issue. And I'm planning to go out myself so it won't be a lie. I have a couple of friends who are planning to go out, but I'm trying to talk them out of it."

"Oh," I say.

I have a question written down about how he'll feel if somebody gets shot, but it doesn't seem like I need to ask it. He says he doesn't want anybody else to go out Deerwalking. That's probably the headline.

"What else?" he asks.

"Actually," I say, "I don't know if you've seen our paper, but it's about this big." I hold out my hands to indicate something narrower than a regular-sized sheet of paper. "I'm probably going to string together every fiftieth word or so to make this an article that will fit." I turn off the recorder. "Thanks."

"Sure," he says.

We walk to the door, which he opens.

"Good luck," I say.

"Thanks."

I'm wondering: Who's the bad guy here? It doesn't seem like Kyle's a bad guy at all. I guess I sort of knew that already. Maybe there isn't any bad guy. Maybe it's whoever put in the "menison" comment. Still, as long as you aren't in a James Bond movie, you don't need a bad guy for bad things to happen.

'I Don't Think Anybody Should be a Deerwalker'

An Interview with Kyle Butler

The Thomson Acres Tribune sat down recently with neighborhood resident Kyle Butler, who is the organizer of upcoming protests against local deer hunting. The following is edited.

TRIBUNE: What first got you interested in the issue of deer hunting?

BUTLER: I've always loved animals and been interested in nature. Through environmental groups, I got to know some people who are involved in overseeing deer hunting for the state.

TRIBUNE: Where did the idea of Deerwalking come from?

BUTLER: A hiking club somewhere in Pennsylvania that organized a Deerwalk for opening day of the hunting season a few years back.

TRIBUNE: What do you say to people who are opposed to Deerwalking?

BUTLER: Here's an analogy. Say your Mother thinks your pet dog has rabies and wants to shoot it. If you know the dog doesn't have rabies, you might stand in front of the dog. You aren't standing there to get shot. You're standing there to make sure the dog doesn't get shot.

TRIBUNE: Would you want me to be a Deerwalker?

BUTLER: I don't want anybody to be a Deerwalker. I just want to be able to say there will be Deerwalkers to discourage the hunters on opening day and get people to think about this issue. And I'm planning to go out myself so it won't be a lie. I have a couple of friends who are planning to go out, but I'm trying to talk them out of it.

[242 words]

"Wait just a my-nute," says Brian. "This is the interview tape and this is the story? How long did you spend on this?"

"I don't know," I say.

"A guess. Give me a guess."

"I don't know," I say.

"You came back from the interview when? Maybe quarter of five? You set the table before dinner, which was at five-thirty. The interview tape is listed here as twenty-three minutes and eighteen seconds."

"Oh. I thought you were giving me a hard time for being slow. You're giving me a hard time for not spending enough time on it. I should have been more careful about going over the tape."

"I'm not giving you a hard time!"

I don't get it. Why is he shouting at me?

"I don't know, all right? When I'm writing something up, I'm not thinking about the time."

It's after dark on Friday night. Brian and Beth and I are sitting shoulder to shoulder in the back seat. Mom and Dad are in front. Dad is driving. It's the classic arrangement. How many hours of our lives have we spent like this? We've been to visit Grandma and Grandpa, Mom's parents. They live maybe half an hour from us. They're nice, but they aren't much like Mom, especially in the way they talk. Mom talks in a cheerful waterfall of language but Grandma and Grandpa talk like the announcers for the golf tournaments that Grandpa likes to watch. Just a few, quiet, well-chosen words, so as not to disturb the golfers.

I wonder sometimes if Grandma and Grandpa don't want to use up too many of their words. There was a kid at my old elementary school who would hardly ever talk. I asked him about it once out on the playground and he told me that he believes that each of us only gets a certain number of words to say in our lifetime. I'm pretty sure he was wrong about that, but I thought it was nice of him to use up some of his words to explain it to me.

We're driving behind some kind of in-between truck. It's bigger than an ordinary pick-up truck but it isn't like a monster truck or anything. There's a word embossed on the tailgate, but I can't tell what it is. The truck stops suddenly and Dad says "Hey!" and jams on the brakes. There are three deer in the road. They look around for just a moment, then one does a step, hop and springs away like Superman flying. Then the other two step, hop and spring away in the same direction. It's like magic. I think: There's no way anybody can walk with the deer.

The word on the tailgate is "READING." It seems like a funny thing to put on a tailgate. I wonder if there are big trucks driving around with "HISTORY" or "MATH" embossed on their tailgates.

When I sit down to write the Mrs. Everett articles, it becomes clear to me that it would be fine to combine them. Why not? Who cares which one is more newsworthy?

Two Discoveries at the Everett House

Alma Everett of 32 Springbrook Drive recently gave the Tribune exclusive permission to photograph two items of interest in her home.

The photograph shows Mrs. Everett holding a picture of her granddaughter with a dog her family got recently. Many of us in the neighborhood remember a dog named Punkin that was a long-time resident of the Everett home. Mrs. Everett reports that the dog in the picture looks exactly like Punkin at that age and has been given the name Punkin Two.

The second shows a full-sized (or larger) statue of Abraham Lincoln created by Mrs. Everett's son, who is an artist. The statue actually sits on the couch in her living room and has a light built into Lincoln's tall hat.

Thank You to Mrs. Everett for allowing us to share these interesting items with our readers!

Now I get to think about the century numbering ditty. What rhymes with 'century'? Mostly made-up words like dentury. (Benchery. Ventury. Wenchery.) I think Lechery is my best bet. It isn't a perfect rhyme, but it's close enough. It has a naughty ring to it, but a disapproving naughty ring that makes it a more likely ditty candidate than, say, Wenchery. What rhymes with 'hundred'? Pretty much nothing. It's worse than 'century'. Maybe Thundered.

We disapprove of lechery-

One ahead for century.
The bison herds once thundered-
One behind for hundreds.

This is getting there. The problem is that it just seems random. Can we connect them? Surely, if Punkin Two and Abraham Lincoln can come together, then lechery and bison herds can come together. Maybe they were issues at the same time.

We disapproved of lechery-
In the Nineteenth Century,
While the herds of bison thundered-
In the Eighteen Hundreds.

I write it on a piece of scrap paper. Above it I write "Ditty for Dad." Below it I write "Or Vice Versa" because it occurs to me that it might work as well or better the other way around. As I put the paper on Brian's desk, my many and pathetic shortcomings come clear to me. God blew the Darren budget on doggerel skills.

Today is Darren McAlpine Day here at Putnam Hills School. Darren was a student here who had a sister with foot problems that meant she had to start wearing clunky boots. Rather than make fun of his sister like most brothers would, Darren and his older brother showed their solidarity with their sister by volunteering to wear similar clunky boots themselves. He loved his sister so much that he was willing to look ridiculous in order to make her feel better. He was willing to have people make fun of him – although, as it turned out, nobody did make fun of him because they realized what a good person he was being. Instead, they looked on him with newfound respect and admiration and the girls at the school all fell in love with him. Eventually the school decided to name a day after him. But he was willing for people to make fun of him, which is the important thing.

My paper-route outfit is a little different this week. I've got a winter jacket instead of the blazer because the weather's getting colder, and I've got chunky black boots with Star Wars stickers on the back because of my sister's feet. As I close in on the DiFuria house, I step with Dark Side authority and my head is full of the tune:

Dum-Dum-Dum-DumDaDum-DumDaDum-

Dum-Dum-Dum-DumDaDum-DumDaDum-

Mrs. DiFuria answers the door.

"Hi," I say. Mr. DiFuria comes around the corner and stands next to Mrs. DiFuria. I don't know which one to talk to. "New edition of the paper," I say to the space in between them. "More on the hunting protests and a feature on Mrs. Everett two houses up."

Mrs. DiFuria looks over at her husband and then back at me. "Sold!" she says to me. "Got any money?" she says to Mr. DiFuria. He disappears.

"Got any news or quotes for us?" I say to Mrs. DiFuria.

She smiles a mystery smile. "Nothing that we're ready to put in the paper yet," she says.

Mr. DiFuria reappears and trades me some coins for a paper.

"Thanks," I say and head off.

What news do they have that isn't ready for the paper yet? I'm thinking this probably means a little DiFuria on the way. Where was the cute, little DiFuria baby girl a dozen years ago?

I don't see a dog in the Carlsen's front yard. There's a track in the grass around the lightpost, which has much of its paint worn off around the bottom foot or so. I wonder if Butchie is inside or if she's buried in the backyard.

Mr. Carlsen answers the door. "Hey," he says. "Doogie Howser!" I hear a noise and then he immediately shuts the door down to a little crack to keep the dog from getting out. "Go away, Butchie! Go away!" he shouts.

"New edition of the paper!" I shout at the door. "More on the protests! Special article about Mrs. Everett next door!"

"Go away, Butchie! You've eaten already!" His nose appears again in the door crack. "How much, again?"

"Fifty cents. Plus fifty cents for last week makes a dollar."

"Just a second," he says and shuts the door.

Why did he say 'You've eaten already'? Did he think Butchie wanted to eat me? Is he messing with me? Is that why he calls me Doogie Howser?

The door opens a few inches and I see the end of a dollar bill coming out. I take it and slide a paper back in its place.

"Thanks," I say and the door closes.

I wait a long time at Mrs. Everett's door because I want to show her the article, but apparently nobody's home. I keep a pen and a pad of little sticky notes in my pocket for when I leave a paper behind. I write:

> *Take a look at page 3!*
> *Darren*

It seems a little corny - like if there was an i I should dot it with a circle or a little heart – but I can't think of a better idea.

The deer-hunting protest march is supposed to leave from the Thomson Acres sign at noon. I'm covering it for the paper. There wasn't a lot of competition for the assignment. When I said I was going, Dad's response was, "Good. Don't go native." That means that I should remember that I'm going as a journalist and not get caught up in the protest.

The march takes place outside of Thomson Acres, so Mom will be there as well, to keep an eye on me. I'm fine with this. She's like my bodyguard for the day – my Secret Service attachment.

The Thomson Acres sign isn't actually in Thomson Acres. It's just outside the original turn in to Thomson Acres, on Hipkins Road. Hipkins is a pretty busy street and doesn't have a sidewalk, so we're going to have to be careful hiking up to the parking lot by the reservoir.

Kyle is waiting by the sign holding a sign of his own, which says "Please Consider Alternatives to Deer Hunting." It doesn't strike me as a very catchy or forceful sign, but it could have been worse. If I were older, I might tease Kyle about not listing all the alternatives to deer hunting on his sign.

Two other teenagers are there. I think I probably saw them at the meeting at the Butlers' house, but I don't know their names.

"Hey," I say to Kyle as Mom and I walk up to the sign.

"Hey," says Kyle to me. "Hey, Mrs. McAlpine."

"We're planning to come along," I say, "but we're not really marchers. I'm covering the march for the paper, and my Mom is covering me."

"Got it," he says. "Thanks for coming."

I ask the other people who they are. Their names are Brock and Madison. They're friends of Kyle and maybe boyfriend and girlfriend with each other. I'm guessing one of them wants to protest deer hunting and the other one sees the march as a kind of date – but I couldn't say which one is which.

A hippie-looking man walks up and asks Kyle if it's OK for him to leave his car on the shoulder of the road. Kyle says it's OK with him, although I'm not sure that's what the man was asking. The man has a ponytail and is wearing some kind of fishing vest with a lot of pockets. I'm thinking he's somebody from one of the environmental groups Kyle has been involved in, but I hear him say he's from the Courant – the real newspaper in the region. He starts to ask Kyle some questions. Kyle, true to form, gives him long and detailed answers, interrupting himself from time to time to give a greeting to somebody walking up to join the group. Eventually, a couple of marchers come to him with a question that requires his attention and he offers to talk more later.

I walk up to the man. "You're with the Courant?" I say.

"Yeah, that's right," he says. "You got a comment you'd like to share?"

I think about saying 'Let me not to the marriage of whatever-it-is admit impediment.'

"I'm actually here covering the march for the Thomson Acres Tribune."

"Oh, man!" he says with a laugh. "The competition just keeps getting younger every year! What's your name?"

"Darren McAlpine."

"Yeah," he says. "I know your Dad. He's been after us on this story for some reason."

"That's my Mom up there," I say, pointing. Mom is talking with Madison about something – maybe about how to get Brock to stand up straight. "She's not a marcher, either. She's here to make sure I don't get run over or kidnapped or something."

He looks around. "So, what's your take on this story?"

I have a few extra copies of the paper in my inside jacket pocket. I pull one out. "Here's today's edition," I say, handing it to him. "We've got an interview with Kyle and an editorial opposing Deerwalking. Have you heard about the Deerwalking?"

"Yeah," he says. "That's the plan to have some of them walk around in the woods after the season opens. Dare the hunters to shoot at them, right?"

"Sort of," I say.

"Seems like a kind of a crazy way to try to get attention," he says.

"Yeah," I say. "I've been hoping they won't do it, but it seems like they might. If you could run a story on it, it might help at least warn the hunters to watch out for them. You know, only so many people read the Thomson Acres Tribune."

"Yeah," he says. "Only so many people read the Courant these days. I don't know what my editors will say about this one. Thanks for the paper."

"Sure."

He leans over to me. "And let me give you just one small piece of advice."

I look up at him.

"Don't spend all your time on this newspaper," he says. "Think about learning to play the banjo. There's a future in the banjo."

We're finally heading up the hill. The guy from the paper has left, but there are maybe ten marchers, not including Mom and me. Meredith Green – Other Darren's sister – is there and comes over to ask how I'm doing, which is nice. No sign of any counter-protesters yet, but maybe there will be some up at the parking lot. I notice that Mom is now walking alongside Kyle. Maybe one of the reasons Mom was willing to come along today is that she wanted to get a word in with Kyle. I walk faster so that I can get close enough to listen in.

"It's not about getting shot," Kyle says. "I promise you I don't want to get shot. However much you don't want to get shot – take that amount and multiply it by a big number and that's how much I don't want to get shot. We just want to get people's attention."

"In a way that's dangerous," says Mom. "And unfair to everyone. Think about some hunter who goes out and thinks he sees a deer going through the woods and shoots it and when he goes up to take a closer look he finds that he's shot some kid who was there on some protest the hunter has never even heard about. Say you're that hunter. How are you going to feel? You are going to feel horrible for the rest of your life!"

"Yes," he says. "It'd be a terrible thing all around. We don't want it to happen. But it shouldn't happen. Hunters aren't supposed to be shooting blindly into the woods. They're supposed to see what they're shooting at. That's part of the point. I'm opposed to people hunting deer because I think there are better options, but if people are going to hunt deer they should see them clearly enough to take them down with a single clean shot. There are rules, you know, about the sizes and genders of the deer you can shoot with a given license. If you can see clearly enough to know if you're shooting at a buck or doe, you ought to be able to see if you're shooting at a deer or a human."

"What could possibly go wrong?" says Mom, getting louder. "Do you know what a hunting trip is for a lot of people? It's a hunting and drinking trip! A weekend out in the woods with your buds and some guns and some booze. I would not want to bet my life that – at a hundred yards away – one of those guys can tell the difference between me and a polar bear!"

"Oh, man," says Kyle. "I really hope you're wrong about that."

"Here's the bottom line for me," says Mom. "People are more important than deer. Maybe that makes me a species fascist, I don't know. I've got nothing against deer. As long as they aren't eating my bushes, I think deer are beautiful creatures. But they aren't as important as people. No deer is worth risking a human life for – any human life – your human life!"

I hear a honk.

"But here's the thing," says Kyle. "If you want to have a discussion, first you've got to get people's attention."

Another honk, getting louder.

Kyle says, "When I talk to-" and then ROAR! WHAM! SQUEAL!

ROAR is a car driving much too fast drifting into the shoulder where we're all walking. Kyle turns and sees it and swings his sign like the car is a hockey puck he can deflect back out to the road.

WHAM is Kyle's sign ricocheting off the car's headlight and knocking Mom over.

SQUEAL is the car zooming away. I can't get a good look at it. It's gone.

I guess this is the hospital, but it's not what you might think of. It's not the hotel part of the hospital or the operating room part of the hospital. It's the hallway full of closet-like little rooms part of the hospital that they call the Emergency Room. Mom is lying down and has a bandage on her head, but she seems to be OK. Everybody is very nice to me, but I don't get a lot of information.

"So how does the bandage make me look?" asks Mom.

"I think it's a good look for you," I say. "It's a little edgy. It's a little bit - you know - in your face."

"Good!"

"It's kind of a tough look," I say. "It's a look that says *'Yes, I have a bandage on my face! You got a problem with that? You want to see what the other guy looks like?'*"

"Excellent!" she says. "I've always wanted that kind of look. I'm thinking it could help me maintain order in the library. *'Don't mess with Quasimodo the Librarian! She pummels disobedient children with her bare face!'*"

"It's too bad that newspaper guy left," I say. "You could have been famous by now."

"That's right. I could be hanging out with all the other famous bandage-faces."

"Sure," I say. "King Tut."

"The Mummy," she says. "The Elephant Man. The Invisible Man."

"I don't know the Invisible Man."

"Of course you don't." she says. "They were old reruns when I was a kid. The Invisible Man wears a dark suit and wraps a cloth around his face when he wants people to know where he is. Then, when he doesn't want people to know where he is, he unwinds the cloth and it looks like there's nothing inside. I think it was considered more appropriate than having the Invisible Man take his pants off."

"Yeah," I say. "I can see that. I mean, not that I can see the Invisible Man."

"So what happens now?"

"We're waiting for more test results."

"If my test results are high enough, do I get to go to Harvard Hospital?"

"Maybe," I say. "How are you at sports?"

We sit for a minute and listen to the various background noises. I went over to Ernie Grondseth's house once, and the place was full of random sound effects because his brothers and sisters were all playing different video or computer games. The emergency room sounds a little like that.

"Here's something interesting," I say.

"What?"

"Know what hit you?"

"It was Kyle Butler's sign, right?"

"It was the top of his sign," I say. "Remember his sign? What almost took your head off was the word 'Please'."

She thinks about this for a bit. "Oh. That's sort of – what?"

I shrug. "Normally, I would have said 'funny'," I say. "Not 'funny – ha-ha. Funny – weird."

"Ironic, maybe. Why? Because it was so rude?"

"Because it hit you. You love Please. You're like the biggest fan that Please has in the world!"

"True enough," she says. "I'd deny it if I could."

"You've spent your whole life telling us how important Please is. Please and Thank You."

"And now it's turned on me. That's what you're saying?"

"Here's the kicker," I say. "'*A little Please and Thank You never killed anybody.*' Who said that?"

"I said that."

"How often?"

"I don't know. Call it a million times."

"And what happened today?"

"A little Please tried to kill me."

I fold my arms. "Is that ironic?"

"Absolutely!" she says. "I think maybe it's ironically ironic." Then: "You know, I should probably keep an eye out for Thank You."

"Hello? Pat?" It's Dad in the hall. He comes in and kneels down by Mom's roller bed and gives her as much of a hug as he can. "Oh, Honey. You OK?"

She starts to cry and can barely talk. "I'm OK," squeaks out. "We're being very brave."
Mom crying makes me cry. I don't understand it, though. I thought we were doing fine joking around when it was just Mom and me.

When things are settled at home, I get a chance to look in on Mom in her bedroom.

"Hi," I say.

"You OK, Kiddo?"

"Yeah."

"Sorry if this was a traumatic day for you."

I'm thinking that she's saying to me all the stuff I should be saying to her.

"I'm sorry you got smashed in the face," I say.

"I'm going to be OK. You know that, right?"

"Yeah. The doctor said you were lucky. Although, I'm thinking if you were really lucky you wouldn't have gotten a sign in your face."

"I was lucky enough."

There's a card and a plant by the bed. "You've had some visitors."

"I have. Grandma came by. Mrs. Butler came by."

"Mrs. Butler?"

"That was kind of weird, actually. She apologized like she was the one who caused the accident, but I'm not sure why. It wasn't her car, and I'm pretty sure she wasn't the crazy person driving it. So how can it be her fault? All I can think is that she knows I was walking there because of Kyle's protest and that Kyle is her son – but that seems crazy to me. I mean, it isn't Kyle's fault that car came so close to us. And even if it were, even if Kyle was the driver of the car, it still wouldn't be Janie's fault. I'm sorry, but you can't hold a mother responsible for everything their kids do. If you become a bank robber, is that my fault? No. I told you not to rob banks, right?"

"Right," I say. "You say that all the time. *'Brush your teeth'* and *'Don't rob banks'*."

"Exactly. So you get a cavity or you rob a bank – that's on you. So, I thought she was crazy for feeling so guilty, but it was nice to see her. We had kind of an argument last time we talked. Maybe that's why she felt guilty. I don't know."

I look at the card. I look at the plant. "I got a question," I say.

"Sure."

"In the hospital, I was thinking that we were both doing OK and feeling OK, kidding around and stuff. And then, when Dad came, all of a sudden we weren't doing OK."

"Yeah. That was kind of weird wasn't it?"

"What happened there?"

She takes a breath. "God's honest truth: I wanted it to be good, even if it wasn't good. When it was just you and me, I felt like I needed to make it good, so that it wouldn't be bad for you. I mean, you aren't a little kid anymore, but you're still my little kid. So when Dad showed up, then it was like I could go off duty. Does that make any sense?"

"Sure."

"Still, you were a big comfort to me when we were hanging out at the hospital. You really were."

"Thanks. Get well."

She reaches up and gives my arm a squeeze. "Thanks," she says. "Good night, Punkin."

"Punkin was Mrs. Everett's dog."

"That's right. I remember Punkin." Mom gives me a little parade wave good night. "Well you can be Punkin Two."

As I'm walking back down the hall, I'm thinking maybe she said *"You can be Punkin, too."*

"It's for you," says Beth. "It's a man from the paper." I pick up the phone. "Hello?"

"Hello, Darren? This is Frank Zimmerman from the Courant. We met this afternoon. You were nice enough to give me a copy of your paper."

"Sure," I say. "I remember."

"I'm just looking to follow up. Your paper gave me some good background on the story. How did the march end up?"

"Not good." I have to stop and take a breath. Something about saying 'not good' to a reporter makes me want to cry. I don't understand it. You'd think I'd be immune to the idea that telling something to a reporter makes it real.

"Why? What happened?"

"A car drove by too fast and hit Kyle's sign and a piece of the sign hit my Mom in the head. She's OK now, but she needed to go to the hospital."

"Oh, wow. I'm so sorry to hear that. Your Mom's OK, though?"

"Yeah, thanks. She's OK."

"OK if I ask a few questions about it?"

"Yeah."

"Do you think it was just an accident or do you think it was related somehow to the protest?"

This is a question I'd been wondering about. "I think it was related," I say. "The car was honking before it hit anything."

"Did the car stop? Do we know who the driver was?"

"No and no."

"Are the police involved?"

"I don't know. I went with Mom to the hospital."

"What's the attitude in the neighborhood towards the protesters?"

"It's all over the map. There's an article with a bunch of quotes in the paper I gave you. The hunters don't like to hear about it. Some people might agree with the protesters' ideas but not agree with tactics like walking around in the woods to see if anyone will shoot them."

"How are things in the area generally? Is there any tension - say between newcomers and old-timers or along racial or ethnic lines?"

"I don't know. I don't have much to compare it to. Seems like most people get along."

"Thanks. I appreciate your time. Is your Dad there?"

"Sure. Just a second."

As I track down Dad - who turns out to be in the kitchen – I think about my inability to answer that last question. He might as well ask me whether our neighbors who are A positive get along with our neighbors who are B negative. I don't know. It's like there's a code that I haven't been able to break. I get the feeling that adults think it's cute that I don't know how to label people, but it just makes me feel stupid.

5. Alice Looks Into the Time Liana Excitedly Called Ron a Zany Yahoo

All Saints Sunday and I'm a civilian. The acolytes on duty miss their cue for the Gospel procession, but they recover pretty quickly and most people probably don't notice.

Mom is home getting better, so Dad brought us today. Dad plays late on Saturday nights and usually only comes to church with us on holidays. I don't know how much Mom needs to stay home to get well and how much Mom wants to stay home because she has a scary-looking bandage on her head. I hope Brian and I don't end up having to show our solidarity with Mom by wrapping our heads in gauze.

The guy delivering the sermon says that the opposite of love is not hate but in fact is fear. Is that right? Is fear the opposite of love? I'm thinking not. Maybe it's true on some psychological or spiritual level, but it's not true at a pretty basic level of what the words mean.

Dad has an expression that I think is lifted from a movie or something because he says it like a cowboy: *'It ain't braggin' if you done it!'* It's pretty catchy but also inaccurate. It is, in fact, only bragging if you've done it. If you haven't done it, then it's lying.

Maybe the preacher's confused about what an opposite is. Maybe what he wants to say is that fear is the thing that works most strongly against love. That could be. That doesn't make it the opposite. The opposite of fat is not exercise. The opposite of fat is skinny.

What about me? I'm fear itself. I worry about pretty much everything. Does that make me the opposite of love? And if I worry about that happening does that make it worse?

So what kind of mistake is it? I like that question. I hate it when Mrs. Featherstone makes us show all our work on a math problem, but I can see the point. You want to know exactly where the train came off the tracks.

Is it a conceptual mistake? Is it a vocabulary mistake? Maybe it's a rhetorical mistake. You stand up to deliver a sermon and you want to make a point. You want to change the way people think about things. But it's hard to change the way people think. We have these models stuck in our heads. So rather than try to change the model, it's easier just to relabel things.

> *That blazing ball of fire you see in the sky during the daytime is not the Sun. No, it's the visible symbol of all our hopes and fears for the future.*

At the end of the service, they say the names of the church members who died since last All Saints Day and ring a bell after each one. There are five names, and for the first time I know a couple of them. Clarence Saunders is Dr. Saunders who walked with a cane and always sat with his wife in the second row, over on the left. Concordia Sadosky was the Candy Lady who would hand out treats after church on holidays.

I look up at the second row, over on the left. A couple of young men are sitting there. I see 23 and 25 Thomson. I think of the missing pool.

Dad is with me but I'm the one who rings the bell. Mr. Johnson opens his door. He looks at us.

"This is my Dad," I say.

"Oh." He looks at Dad. "He's your kid?"

"Yeah."

Mr. Johnson nods and addresses himself to Dad. "He's not too bad. Compared to all the other kids you see these days – he's not so much of an idiot."

Dad nods. "Thanks." Then, "I think maybe that's the nicest thing anybody's ever said about him."

I think they're joking – but maybe also competing in some kind of a Deadpan Smackdown.

Mr. Johnson looks over at me then back to Dad. "You want to make sure I'm not a creep, right?"

"Right. And also that he's not bothering you."

"He's not bothering me. He's been a good help actually if you can believe it. And I'm kind of an idiot, but I'm not a creep. If it's OK with you, I'd like him to help me a little more today. I won't keep him too long. I know he's got stuff to do."

"Good," says Dad and he turns around. "See you later."

As we head to Mr. Johnson's den, he says, "What does your Dad do?"

"He plays the banjo."

He thinks about this for a moment. "You don't often meet people these days who has a useful skill."

I think about correcting his grammar, but decide to let it pass. He's not looking for me to copy edit his speech.

"What about you?" I say. "What do you do?"

He sits at his computer. "Retired. I used to machine jet engine parts."

"Oh. Cool."

"I got out at a good time," he says. "It's not the job it used to be. Machinist today is an office job. They're sitting at a computer all day. Running a machine tool used to be like playing a musical instrument. Maybe a little like playing the banjo."

He has another email to his daughter for me to review. It needs some polishing, but it's better than his previous one. I stop for a moment to consider the following:

Don't knock yourself too hard. Try and forget about it.

"What is it?" he asks.

"We could make this more correct, but I'm not sure I want to."

"Why?"

"I like the way this reads. It sounds like you."

"[Darn] it!" he says. "I don't want it to sound like me! I want it to be correct!"

So I have him change it to:

Don't knock yourself so hard. Try to forget about it.

When we get to the end of the email, he says, "I got some good news."

"What?"

"The company is replacing that pellet stove under warranty. No cost to me."

"That's great!"

"Of course, they ought to replace it. Lifetime warranty and the thing gets a big crack when it's less than a year old. Anyway, we're square. You been a big help, but you don't owe me any more of your copy editing. Now go enjoy the afternoon."

Before I leave, I ask him about Deerwalking.

"I don't know about that," he says, "but you know who disrupts hunters the most?"

"Who?"

"Other hunters. There are these [stupid] hunters who roar around in the woods on these ATVs. Sounds like a motorcycle gang's coming around the corner. I was out hunting once on state land west of the reservoir. I got up before dawn and hiked in for three hours and could just see a couple of bucks off in the distance when the roar started up and before long some clown pulled up and says to me: *Seen anything?* Well – yes, actually, there was something to see before you roared up on your stupid trail Harley."

As usual, I'm the last one to arrive at the Sunday dinner table. Mom is sitting at her place in a bathrobe, with reams of gauze wrapped around the top of her head. Dad appears to be on duty and not his usual, relaxed self.

"Special treat!" he announces. "McAlpine's Marvelous Mess!"

Dad has a limited repertoire of meals he can make. He can cook up a special kind of broiled hot dogs. He can do macaroni and cheese from a box. And then there's McAlpine's Marvelous Mess, which is a kind of toasted cheese sandwich with pimento olive bits mixed in. It's the most popular of his dishes, but that may be because of the name.

"OK," says Dad when I'm seated. "Let's start with grace." And he bows his head and says our Grace.

"Amen!" We all say. I look over at Brian and wonder if it was Dad's turn.

The plate of Marvelous Mess starts to get passed around. "I can make more if we need it! Also, we've got baby carrots in this dish and grapes in that dish!"

I think about making a wisecrack about the side dishes. Baby carrots and grapes? I like both of them, but their presence on the table suggests that Dad was focused on grilling up the Marvelous Mess slices and then realized that it would be a good idea to have some side dishes when it was about thirty seconds before dinner time.

On the other hand, he's filling in and keeping us fed and there's Mom sitting up and looking brave. So I keep my mouth shut and help myself.

"Brian!" says Dad. "What's new in your world?"

Brian looks around, grabs some baby carrots out of the dish and sets three of them in a row on his placemat, in front of his plate. "Bing! Bing Bing!" He indicates them with a theatrical wave of his arm. "This week I learned about the Monty Hall Paradox."

We look at his carrots. "That's nice, Honey," says Mom.

"What is it?" asks Beth.

"It's a logic puzzle based on an old game show. There are three doors. Door Number One. Door Number Two. Door Number Three." He holds up each carrot in turn. I guess they're supposed to be the doors. "Behind one door is a beautiful new car."

"Can you use a different example?" says Mom.

"What?"

"A different example. I don't like cars this week."

"Sure. Behind one door is a luxurious round-the-world cruise."

"Much better," says Mom.

"Behind the other two doors are goats."

"Goats?" says Beth.

"Ugly, mean goats."

"I like goats."

"Behind the other two doors are spiders."

"Ugh!"

"So the idea here is that you don't want to pick a door with a spider behind it. You want to pick the one with the luxurious cruise. OK, Beth, you pick. Door One. Door Two. Door Three."

She studies the carrots carefully.

"Door One," she says.

"What about the rest of us?" I ask. "Do we get to pick?"

"No. Only one contestant allowed. So Beth has picked Door Number One. But before I tell her if she has a cruise or a spider, I tell her something else. I say – *'Hey , Beth. Let me show you something. Look at this. Door Number Two has a spider behind it.*

Good thing you didn't pick that one! All right now. Do you want to stay with Door Number One or switch to Door Number Three?'"

Brian eats Door Number Two while Beth studies the remaining carrots.

"Stay," she says.

"You're staying with Door Number One?"

"Yes!"

Brian looks around. "Should she switch?"

Mom looks at Dad. Dad looks at me.

"It shouldn't matter, right?" I say.

"Maybe it shouldn't matter," he says. "Or maybe that's why it's called a Paradox. The answer is that Beth should switch. She had a one in three chance of winning with her first choice – but because the other option was eliminated she now has a two in three chance of winning if she switches."

"Is that right?" says Dad.

"We can try it after dinner," says Mom. "Only we'll need to get a bunch of cruises and spiders."

I'm thinking about what it'd be like to be on that game show. "Man," I say. "It would be horrible to switch and then have Door Number One be the winner."

Beth looks at Brian. "So did I win?"

"Probably not. But it's OK. You got a friendly, magical spider, like in *Charlotte's Web*."

This seems to satisfy her.

"Monty Hall?" I say.

"It's the name of the guy," says Brian.

"He was the announcer," says Dad. "Great announcer voice!" he says in a pretty good announcer voice. "Did you ever see the movie *Happy Gilmore*?" He looks around but nobody responds. "It's one of the top ten hockey-player-becomes-a-professional-golfer comedies. Anyway, Monty Hall is in the movie, playing himself."

I'm still trying to work out the problem. Why should it be any different to pick a door as a switch choice than if I had picked it as my first choice? It's still the same door.

"Darren got a mention in Frank Zimmerman's article in today's paper," says Dad. I get a bit of golf applause for this. "What else is new with you?"

"I've been working on missing pets," I say. "It's sort of a research project. It seems to me like we get a lot of missing pets in this neighborhood. I came up with 11 known lost pets over the past year. That's a combination of missing pet reports we've had in the paper plus some other cases I remember where people were putting up signs or asking around."

"Yeah. That's a lot," says Dad. "Eleven."

"So Brian and I did a follow up on our rounds yesterday. We didn't get to everybody, but we got to a lot and it seems like there are four cases where the pet was found. So seven unexplained disappearances." I look around. "I made a map."

"I love maps," says Mom.

I run to my room and grab the map and then run back. It's kind of corny, but I glued the map to a big piece of construction paper so I can hold it up, which I now do.

"This is Glenbrook here. This is us. Thomson's up this way. Deepwood's down here. The seven red circles are the unexplained missing pets. The numbers in the circles are the order the pets went missing."

Dad gets up to come around between Beth and Brian and get a better look at the map.

"Verrry Eenteresting!" says Brian.

"That's us?" asks Beth, pointing.

"Yeah."

"So," says Dad. "Have you figured it out? Do you have a theory?"

Brian points and waves his hand around. "If you connect the dots, it spells: 'SURRENDER DOROTHY!'"

"Wrong alphabet," says Dad. "It says: 'First we take the Earthlings' pets...'"

Mom leans in. "If they were all on the far side of Springbrook, I'd say it was critters coming down from the woods." She points from one side of the map to the other. "If they were all on the far side of Glenwood, I'd say it was the speeding traffic on Hipkins." She stops and looks around at us. "A subject – may I say – on which I am now a notable expert."

"It's Mrs. Waldron," says Beth.

We all stop and look at her. Mrs. Waldron is a nice lady a little older than my folks. She lives on Glenwood, which is part of Brian's route.

Beth looks around at us staring at her. "What?" she says. "It's a nice map, but you should have just asked me. I could have told you. It's Mrs. Waldron."

"What do you mean?" I ask.

"She doesn't say so, but people know. Kara lives across the street from her, and she knows. Mrs. Waldron doesn't like to see people take bad care of their pets. If she thinks people aren't being good to their pets, they just disappear."

"The pets, you mean?" I say. "She kidnaps them?"

"Maybe. They disappear. I think Mrs. Waldron has some nephews or something that take care of the details."

"The pets that get taken," says Brian. "Where do they go?"

"Mrs. Waldron has friends."

"The original rescue dogs," says Dad.

I take the map off the table and lean it against the wall. Dad goes back to his place. "I don't know," he says. "Is that fair?"

"It's fair if Mrs. Waldron is right," says Mom. "It's not so good if she's wrong."

"I think it's fair sometimes," says Beth. "I think Mrs. Waldron's nephews should kidnap the Pinkerton's dog. They're mean to that poor dog."

It strikes me that her comment about the Pinkerton dog is not a random thought. Beth is somehow on this case. She's doing something about it. Maybe she's talked to her friend who knows Mrs. Waldron or maybe she's written a note to Mrs. Waldron.

> *Dear Mrs. Waldron,*
> *If you aren't too busy, please have your nephews kidnap*
> *the Pinkerton's dog.*
> *Sincerely yours,*
> *Beth McAlpine*
> *P.S. Hurry!*

Dad looks over at Mom. "What about you, Patrice? Anything new for you this week?"

Mom sits up and gives a toothpaste commercial smile. "It's been a very quiet, uneventful week for me," she says. "Hiking around the neighborhood, visiting at the hospital. In fact, just to keep it that way, I've decided to take this week off from work, stay home, watch some soap operas, eat bon-bons."

"It's funny you should say that," says Dad, "because I was thinking the same thing. I think I'll stay home this week, see if I can hang around the place enough to annoy our children. Cramp their style."

This is no small step for Dad. Librarians still get paid when they take days off but banjo players don't.

"So, if that's it..." says Dad.

"What about me?" says Beth.

"I'm sorry! I'm sorry! You did such a nice job telling us about Mrs. Waldron that I forgot to ask you about your news. So, Beth—what's new in your world?"

She looks around to make sure she has our attention. "Miss Squirrel and Mr. Bear have set a date. They're getting married next Sunday."

Whack fall the daddy-o!
Whack fall the daddy-o!
Whack fall the daddy-o!
There's whiskey in the jar!

I think this is the Overthinking Department, but Dad is playing his ukulele and singing. Maybe it's because he hasn't performed for a few days. He looks up at us and strums.

Oh, welcome to the Overthinking Department-
The Overthinking Department is the road to ride-
(although it's not really a road-)
Oh, welcome to the Overthinking Department-
And if you want to ride it, got to ride it like you find it-
Get your ticket at the station-
(although we don't actually have a station-)
(I think maybe it's a metaphor-)
For the Overthinking Department!

This was more or less to the tune of a song called *Rock Island Line*. Brian and I applaud. "Thank you, thank you," says Dad. "I'm here all week. Be sure to tip your waitress. So what do we have?"

"How do we cover our own Mom being hit by a car?" says Brian. "Also, can we do a story on Mrs. Waldron?"

"D-day for Deerwalking," I say. "Hunting season starts on Saturday. Also, I'm wondering if there was any damage from Halloween."

"Escalators," says Dad. "And next Friday."

I bite. "What's next Friday?"

"Exactly!" says Dad. "What does it mean? If I say *'Let's have lunch next Friday?'* when do I want to have lunch?"

"Next Friday?"

"Lucky guess! OK, let's look at a calendar. Where are we? Here we go." He holds out a little planner book. "Today is Monday, November sixth. Is next Friday November tenth - the next day that is a Friday? Or is the tenth This Friday - and Next Friday is November seventeenth - Friday of next week?"

"Next Friday is Friday of next week - the seventeenth," says Brian.

"No," I say. "Next Friday is the next Friday - the tenth."

Brian looks at me. "No, no, no, no! You're kidding right?"

"I have never been more serious! Next Friday is the tenth!"

Brian looks sadly over to Dad. "Where did we go wrong?" he says.

Dad holds up his hands – one of which is still holding the ukulele. "Don't assume I'm in your camp. I'm agnostic on this one. It could be either one." He pulls out a Tribune, folded back to one of the inside pages. "The reason I bring this up is that I was belatedly noticing this story from last week." He points to the following item:

Tag Sale Planned

Janet Luebker will be holding a tag sale at her home, 26 Springbrook Drive, on Saturday, November 11th starting at 9 am. There will be a preview next Friday at 6 pm.

I wrote that and thought it seemed pretty clear at the time. Whatever you think 'next' means, the preview has to be Friday the 10th. Still, I can see Dad's point.

"Guilty as charged," I say. "I'll watch out for that. And what was it about escalators?"

"OK," says Dad. "I was in a big parking garage in West Hartford last week, and there were escalators going up and down - that is, there was one set of escalators connecting to the next floor down and another set of escalators connecting to the next floor up. And each set of escalators has one side going up and the other side going down. Right?"

"Hold on," says Brian. "Darren wants to make a map."

"No point," I say. "Whatever the question is - just ask Beth."

"So here's the deal," says Dad. "I'm thinking I need a better vocabulary for describing escalators. Because all I've got is Up Escalator and Down Escalator and here in this parking garage that's ambiguous. Does Up Escalator mean the escalator that I can use to go up to the next floor or does it mean the escalator someone else can use to come up from the floor below?"

If I'm a parrot sitting on my shoulder, I want to go choke myself on a cracker. Who cares about naming escalators? But I'm not that parrot. I love this stuff.

"Hold on," says Brian. "If I say 'Up Escalators' plural - does that mean all the escalators going up or does it mean the bank of escalators going to the next floor up, including the down side?"

"So," I say, "on any given floor, you need four names. One for the Up-Up escalator, one for the Up-Down escalator, and then two more for Down-Up and Down-Down."

Dad starts strumming and sings:

>*When you're alone and life is making you lonely you can always go...*

He holds out his hands and we stare at him dumbly. He sighs and continues alone:

>*Down-Down!*

"You've never heard that? Petula Clark? *Downtown*? What are they teaching in the schools these days?"

"Try it again," I say.

He smiles and strums:

>*When you're alone and life is making you lonely you can always go...*

And we all shout:

>*Down-Down!*

"Much better!" he says. "OK, I have one other thing. I'm thinking this might be a good bye week." Bye week means we don't put out a newspaper. "Start to aim now for a week from Saturday."

"Next Saturday," says Brian.

"A week from next Saturday," I say. "Why?"

Dad shrugs. "We've got an invalid in the house. We've done several weeks in a row. And I figure we'll want an edition the following week to report on Opening Day for hunting season, even if hopefully nothing at all happens. So think about it, anyway. Meanwhile, we have Brian's interesting question. How – if at all – do we cover what happened to your Mom?"

"I have a connection to the family," says Brian. "I think I could get an interview."

"Watch out for the older brother," I say. "I hear he's a piece of work."

"Do we want an article about what happened to your Mom?"

Brian and I look at each other. "Maybe," I say. "I'll take a shot at it and we can decide." I start to write it in my head.

Sometimes the News Hits Close to Home

by Darren McAlpine

On Saturday, November 4, I was covering the deer-hunting protest march up Hipkins Road. My mother, Patrice McAlpine, had come along – not as a protester, but because I was there. Shortly before 1 pm, we heard a honk and a roar. A car, traveling north on Hipkins, was going much too fast and too close to the marchers to be safe. It was a black Jeep.

"Darren?"

"It was a black Jeep," I say.

Dad looks at me funny. "Does that mean Yes or No?"

"What's the question?"

"Article about Mrs. Waldron?"

"Maybe," I say, "but listen to this. I was just thinking about what we might write about Mom getting hit in the head, and I got a picture in my head. The car was a black Jeep."

"The car that hit your Mom?"

"Yeah, but it didn't actually hit Mom. It hit Kyle's sign that hit Mom."

"You getting anything else? A license plate? A bumper sticker?"

"No."

"How about a model?"

"I don't know."

"Look up Jeep models. Google it. See if you can tell model and year."

I'm in my pajamas and robe, reading in the living room when the bell rings. I answer the door and it's a woman who seems vaguely familiar. She's small for a grown-up – not much taller than I am. She seems surprised to see me.

"Oh? I'm just..." She stops for a moment. "Is Karl... Is Mr. McAlpine there?"

I step back into the living room. "Dad?"

Dad comes in from the hall and follows me to the door.

"Deena," he says when he sees her.

"I'm sorry about..." she says. "I was worried. I didn't know what was, you know..."

Dad is clearly uncomfortable about this short woman who doesn't finish her sentences. He looks around. I wonder if I should disappear somehow.

"Right," he says. "It's late for a visit. Here – I'll walk you to your car." He grabs a coat off a hook in the entryway and looks over at me. "Have you brushed your teeth?"

"Yeah."

"Good. I'll be right back." He steps out and closes the door. Pretty soon I can hear them talking outside in hushed voices. Some of the things Deena says are loud enough that I can make them out.

"I was so worried!" she says.

"It's just for now, that's all it is," she says.

"I love you so much!" she says.

Deena I remember is a bartender at the Peabody Inn. Why are Deena and Dad having such an urgent-sounding conversation in our driveway? Why was she worried and why does she love him so much? This could be something horribly bad. I don't want to think it but I can't help myself. Maybe Dad is cheating on Mom with this woman from his work. I feel dizzy. I'm Pippin, wishing I hadn't looked into the palantir, the seeing stone. My life teeters. None of us is safe. Saruman knows now where I live.

Is Deena sexy in some way that Mom isn't? I try to replay her picture, but I don't get much. Mostly I get Short. I don't think of Mom as sexy, but I always assumed that was just a family thing. Nobody thinks their Mom is sexy, but she must be or she wouldn't be a Mom.

Dad is still talking to Deena in the driveway. I get a song in my head, making fun of me.

> *Someone's in the driveway with Deena,*
> *Someone's in the driveway I know-oh-oh-oh-*
> *Someone's in the driveway with Deena,*
> *Strummin' on the old banjo.*

This is potentially the end of everything about my life that I like. Mom'll be angry and depressed. Dad'll move out. We'll see him on alternate weekends, when Brian and Beth and I will crowd into some apartment where he and Deena are living and none of us will know what to say to one another. Mom will have to sell the house and we'll move away from our friends and maybe have to go to a new school where everyone will hate me and make fun of these stupid shoes.

I shouldn't keep standing in the entryway. I should just go to bed. Only going to bed means looking in on Mom and saying Good Night and Mom will look me in the eyes and see what I'm not saying to her. *Dad is out on the driveway talking with his girlfriend.* I can't do that, so maybe I just go quietly to bed as an accessory to the crime.

Dad comes back in. "Sorry about that," he says. "Shouldn't you be in bed now?"

"Yeah," I say. "Good night." I start for the hall, then turn back. "Say Good Night to Mom for me."

I can't sleep, so I get up, sit at my desk, take a piece of scrap paper and write:

> *Walter has oranges in September. Doug eats egg nog artichokes in September. Doug ate David's big eggplant in November. Gavin bit a dog.*

I turn off my light, tiptoe down the hall, and slip the paper under Brian's door. His light is off. As I tiptoe back, I hear Mom and Dad arguing about something. I can't hear the words and don't want to. I go back to my room and climb into bed.

It's late. I look at my clock. One-one-one-one.

There's a game I play sometimes where you have all these cars in a tight parking lot and you have to figure out how to shuffle them all around to free a certain red car that's usually trapped way in the back. One of the things that makes it tricky is that, looking down on it, some of the cars are aimed up and down and some are aimed left and right.

I'm thinking about that game in math class today because there's a lockdown and we're all sitting on the floor of a closet being quiet. We're packed pretty tight and some of us are facing front or back and some of us are facing left or right. If the red car is Jonah Regner, sitting in the back corner of the closet, I'm losing the game for sure.

Becca Hennessey is one row ahead of me and two rows to my left – a knight move away.

I think the lockdown is just a drill. Mrs. Featherstone seems unworried and a little annoyed by the whole thing. Still, I picture the terrorist gunman running into the empty classroom and considering the different doors he could look behind. Door Number One or Door Number Two or Door Number Three?

155

He advances towards Door Number One, but then the announcer tells him that there are no kids behind Door Number Two. Does he want to change his guess?

Of course he should change his guess. It'd double his chances. I wonder if I should have used this argument with Kyle. It's mathematically proven that changing your mind is better than sticking with your original plan.

But I don't want the terrorist to double his chances. That is, unless this closet we're sitting in is behind Door Number One.

After school, I go with Dad to run an errand at a big hardware store. Dad wants to get storm windows to go over the basement windows in our house. He gives the measurements to a clerk who disappears and Dad and I stand leaning against a display counter waiting. We both look down the aisle towards the back of the store and see a man and woman walking slowly in our direction. The woman looks pretty normal but the man has a beard and is carrying over his shoulder a large, wooden cross. It looks to me like Mr. and Mrs. Jesus. Dad give me a "That's different!" look.

When I got home from school today, there was a note on my desk:

> *Ivan thinks his idea needs knowledge. Dave eats every nice avocado in Seattle. Alice looks into the time Liana excitedly called Ron a zany yahoo.*

This made me feel a little better. Maybe Deena is like a grown-up Lucille. Maybe Dad is too nice to hang up on her. Of course, when I don't hang up on Lucille, I also don't have a wife and three kids at home.

The couple stops just a few feet away from us. Mrs. Jesus looks at paint swatches while Jesus carefully moves the cross off his shoulder and rests it against some tall shelving.

"Looks heavy," says Dad.

He looks over at us. "It is heavy," he says. "And awkward."

I try to think what I should say to Jesus, but all I can think of is, "I thought you would be taller," which I don't say out loud.

"Would you like a hand?" asks Dad.

"I can get it out to the car," he says. Then he smiles. "Now, if you want to come dig the hole for it..." And he puts the cross back on his shoulder and he and Mrs. Jesus head down the aisle toward the checkout.

The clerk comes back with options for the storm windows, and I take a minute to go to the back of the store and see if they really sell crosses here. What they sell that look like crosses are mailbox posts. I guess the bottom part has to go into a pretty deep hole, because they look a lot taller than the mailbox posts you see by the side of the road.

This is the Gospel for the afternoon: *If you would be my disciple, take up your mailbox post and carry it out to the car.*

I'm working on a Language Arts paper at my desk in my room. My working title is *Cassandra: the First Journalist.* She had this very interesting curse where she'd be able to predict the future – especially bad things that are going to happen – but nobody would believe her. You'd think it'd discourage her and she'd stop warning people, but that's not how the story goes. She keeps on warning and warning and warning, like it's her job.

I was a little reluctant to pick Cassandra for my report because usually guys only do reports about guys. I think she's a good subject for me, though, and I think the teacher is going to eat it up.

I look up and there's Brian. He almost never comes in my room. He's holding a paper tube.

"Hey," I say.

"Hey," he says, "I wanted to give you a heads-up about something."

"OK. Shoot."

"This is probably going to be my last semester doing the paper."

Oh, man, I think. That's it. There's no paper without Brian. I'm eleven years old and I just got laid off. Why is he quitting? Is it my fault? Maybe he's just tired of it. Maybe he wants to spend more time on his music. How long has he been planning this? What am I going to do instead of the paper? Who am I if I'm not doing the paper? I don't know – I'm less than I was five minutes ago. My obituary just got shorter. My career as a journalist soon to be forgotten, just another built-over swimming pool.

> *Darren was a sixth grader at Putnam Hills School. Period, full stop.*

"Oh," I say. I stare at him, trying to keep a poker face. I don't want him to know that I'm disappointed. Maybe he has to stop. He couldn't do it forever. "Does that mean – like – the end of the year?"

"Yeah," he says. "I was going to say this was my last year doing the paper, but I thought that might be ambiguous. You might expect that to mean academic year rather than calendar year."

"Good call. That's what I would have thought." I think about asking more questions, but I'm not sure I want to know the answers. I decide on a diversionary tactic. "You could have said Next January," I say. "You're going to stop working on the paper Next January."

"I'm going to stop This January. Next January is a year after that."

"That's crazy. Are you telling me that the next January is not Next January?"

"Yes, Dalrymple! You are the only person in captivity who doesn't understand This and Next. The one coming up is This. The one after that is Next."

I stand up at this. "Poppycock!" I'm not sure if this means anything, but Dad says it sometimes when he disagrees with something. "This is the one going on right now. This Week is right now. Next Week is the one after that, the one that is next. There is no January happening right now, and therefore it makes no sense to say This January. The upcoming January will be the next month to be a January and is therefore referred to as Next January."

"How about this – We're doing the paper through December? At least I am. You might want to think about keeping it going on your own – or just retire early and write your memoirs."

He makes a sweeping gesture with his arms and I point at the tube in his hand. "What's that?"

"In honor of the occasion, a small thank you from your brother. You can hang this on your wall or sell it for millions on EBay." He hands me the tube, which I unroll like a big scroll. It's his poster of Robert Redford and Dustin Hoffman as newspaper reporters. I guess it's my poster now. I've always loved this poster, but what I loved about it was that it was on Brian's wall.

I feel like I'm not doing a very good job getting information about what's going on. Maybe I've already stopped being Deputy Editor. Brian leans his mouth close to my ear.

"This is your time," he says. "Do everything."

I'm in the backyard with Other Darren. We're throwing a ball back and forth with lacrosse sticks. Usually, we suck at this, but today for some reason we're catching and throwing the ball like pros. Wormtongue appears on our back porch and throws a seeing stone down on us. It looks a little like a Magic 8 Ball – shiny and black and round. I try not to look at it, but I can hear that it's ticking like a bomb about to explode. I run over and scoop it up into the netting of the stick and, in a single fluid motion, launch the stone high over our back fence, up the hill and into the Schipkes' pool. Other Darren and I stand for a moment looking up at the spot and then: "KA-WHOOSH!" The explosion sends water up into the air and blows a hole out the side of the pool, and now a rain of pool water is coming down from the sky and a torrent of water is pouring out the hole and down the hill into our yard. I feel the drops on my face and the rising water on my ankles and I think: *I've got to wake up now or I'll wet the bed.*

Do everything. What does that mean? Does it mean I should go crazy? Take drugs and rob banks? Maybe, but I'm thinking probably not. Probably it's meant to be encouraging. Something like: *You can do more than you think. Now go out and do it.*

Kyle answers the door. "Hey," he says.

"Hey," I say.

"How's your Mom?"

"Good."

"Sorry I swung that sign at the car."

"That's OK."

"Good job writing up that interview."

"Thanks."

"What's up?"

"I want another interview."

"Sure. Why not? You want to come in?"

He stands aside but I don't move.

"Actually," I say, "you know what would be good? I'd like to interview you walking around in the woods where you'll be Deerwalking on Saturday. If you're still planning to do that."

Kyle thinks about this. "OK, I guess. Maybe I could get my Mom to take us out there later this week. I can't drive you out there myself because I've just got a learner's permit and can't drive with any kids in the car."

"I'm not sure it'll work later in the week," I say. This is not quite a lie because I'm just saying I'm not sure, which is true about anything. I'm not sure the sun will come up tomorrow morning. "Do you have like a family friend or relative in the area who could drive us?"

Kyle stares over my head for a few moments, then pulls out his phone, scrolls through a menu and hits a button. "Hey," he says. "Any chance you could give me and a kid I know a ride for a kind of an errand? I don't know – half and hour, an hour maybe. Yeah – now if you can. Great. Thanks a lot." He looks up at me. "Five minutes. Come in for a sec while I grab a snack and get a coat."

I step in and he shuts the door. "Can I use your phone to let my folks know?"

"Sure." He hands me his cell phone. I dial our home number. Dad picks up.

"Hey-ello," he says.

"This is Darren. I'm over at the Butlers. I'm going to interview Kyle again, only this time we're getting a ride over to the state forest so I can interview him where he's planning to be Deerwalking on Saturday."

"Good idea," he says. "Take some photos. The Money Shot would be Kyle with a deer - but a good shot would be Kyle with a state forest sign."

"Just a second," I say. I cover the phone and look over at Kyle. "Who's going to drive?"

"I have an older cousin who lives in the area. Jeff."

"Jeff what? Where does he live?"

"Jeff Heminway – like the writer only not quite. He's out of college and works nights. He lives in the River Bend complex."

I talk into the phone again. "Did you get that? A responsible adult relative driving us just up to the reservoir and back. All right? I'll be home by dinner time."

"See you then," says Dad.

I'm disappointed when Jeff drives up in a yellow Subaru. I guess maybe it would have been too easy if he'd driven up in a black Jeep. Still, I like easy. Why does everything have to be hard? Kyle and I go out and hop in his car. I sit in back.

"This is Darren," says Kyle.

Jeff gives me a quick look in the rear-view mirror. "Hi, Darren."

"He and his brother write the neighborhood paper. He wants to interview me up at the state park. If you can just drive us up Hipkins and into the parking lot for the reservoir."

"Sure." He backs out and heads down the street.

"Darren's Mom was the one that got hit in the head."

"How'd that happen?"

"During the march. I told you about it. That car came too close and I hit my sign against it."

Jeff doesn't say anything.

Pretty soon we're on Hipkins, heading up the hill. "It was right there," I say.

Jeff doesn't take his eyes off the road. "Which side?" he asks.

Being a newspaper reporter is like being a poker player. You learn to tell when people are bluffing. When Jeff says "Which side?" and doesn't look either way, that seals it for me. He's playing dumb. There's a big shoulder on the right and almost no shoulder on the left. It's obvious where the march must have been.

The downside of being a reporter is that you can't necessarily call the bluff. If someone tells you a lie, sometimes you just have to print it.

> *"We had a great time visiting our relatives in the Buffalo area!" says Mr. Fandell.*

I try to aim my voice up towards Kyle. "What happened after my Mom and I got driven off to the hospital?"

"What?" says Jeff.

"It's a question for Kyle. What happened after we left? Did you finish the march?"

"No," says Kyle. "I thanked people for coming out but called off the rest of the march. At that point we didn't know how serious it was with your Mom."

"Sure," I say. "Do you know if anybody was up where the march was supposed to end? Were there any supporters or counter-protesters up there, where we're headed now?"

"I don't know. We never got up here." We turn off Hipkins and onto the little road that leads to the parking lot. "Brad came up that morning. Just to check out where we should go. We were going to end the march right at the beginning of the parking lot. There's a little bit of a hill there and we figured we could stand up there and make a couple of speeches." He looks over at Jeff. "Keep going through to the back lot. We're not walking around the reservoir. We're heading into the state forest land."

There are always a lot of cars parked in the area for the reservoir. Further back, the lot with access to the state forest has a few cars in it but is more open. Jeff pulls us into a space. "I'll wait here," he says.

Kyle and I get out. I knock on Jeff's window and he lowers it.

"Does your phone get a signal up here?" I ask.

He pulls out his phone and checks. "Yeah."

"And is your phone linked to Kyle's phone?"

"I don't know. What does that mean?" He looks over at Kyle. "Is my phone linked to yours?"

"Beats me."

I stay focused on Jeff. "Your whatever-he-is – your cousin over here – next Saturday – actually I call it next Saturday, you may call it this Saturday – anyway, just a few days from now – he's planning to wander around in these large and – at that time – hunter-infested woods – and it's possible that he could get lost or need help. If you go to your Find My Phone app there's a way to link your phones together so that you can find him. OK? It's like his phone is a homing beacon. OK? Let's try it."

Kyle pulls out his phone and it takes a few minutes but they find the right app and get their phones set up so they can find each other. I figure it can't hurt. I'm relieved that it seems to work and that they were willing to do it. I was thinking I might lose them when I started rambling about this Saturday and next Saturday.

We leave Jeff sitting in the car and head toward the main trail. I use my pod to take a picture of Kyle next to a sign by the entrance. No deer appear behind him, but it's still a pretty good shot. Then I turn on the recorder app. We start hiking in. It's a paved trail at this point.

"So you're still planning to do this – go Deerwalking?" I say.

"Yeah, but the point is not me being brave or crazy or whatever. The point is to draw attention to the problems with deer hunting and the fact that there are good alternatives."

"That car that came so close to you and hit your sign. You think that was some kind of counter-protest? You think somebody was trying to scare you?"

We walk a while before Kyle says anything. "I don't know what that was. Sorry if it had anything to do with me. But, you know – if it was supposed to scare us away, that's all the more reason to keep up the protest."

"Maybe," I say. It's my Dad's "you're wrong" kind of Maybe.

"Why? Who do you think did it?"

"I have a theory but I'd rather not say yet. Is anyone else coming with you? What about Brad?"

"Brad's very gung-ho. He'll probably lead the way."

"And are you doing this just once?"

"Opening Day," he says.

There are some other people around, mostly walking dogs or running. I don't understand running significant distances on purpose. When I have to run more than about a minute, I feel like I'm being tortured. I've heard that when people do it enough, they start to enjoy the pain. This just seems unhealthy to me. It makes me think of messed up girls cutting themselves or grown-ups deciding they like cooked spinach. Does running build muscles? Maybe. Steroids build muscles and nobody says those are healthy for you.

The pavement bends to the left, but we go straight on an unpaved path that heads up a hill.

"See any deer?" I ask. "My Dad says the Money Shot is you with a deer."

"Money Shot?"

"Not a shot like a gunshot." I feel bad now about using that term. "It means a photo. It'd be cool to have a photo of you with a deer."

"Keep your eyes open, but don't hold your breath." He stops and makes a motion. "I mean, look around at all the deer! You can see why we need to hunt them. They've gotten so overpopulated here!" He's being sarcastic, but it seems a little forced. He's a pretty earnest guy. I don't think he gets a lot of practice being sarcastic.

At the top of the hill, we turn around. There's a little bit of a view back towards the parking lot and over to the reservoir. It's very peaceful looking. The reservoir isn't scary when you're looking down at it. This hill might be dangerous on Saturday, but it feels like the safest place in the world right now.

"Say you come out here on Saturday and something terrible happens." I look over at Kyle. "Say you get shot and killed. Do you have a message you'd want to pass on? What do you want people to remember?"

"Downer question!" He stares out over the trees. Somewhere below us, between the parking lot and the river, is Thomson Acres. "Sorry it didn't work out," he says. "This wasn't the plan. Love to my family. Thanks to my friends."

I'm not sure what he's talking about, but decide he's answering the question. *This is my time*, I think. Maybe. Or maybe I'm Connor claiming to own the night.

I pull out my pod and turn off the recorder. "You know," I say. "This is B.S."

"What do you mean?"

"You aren't going to stop a single hunter and there's a chance you could get shot. It's a lousy plan." He's about to reply, but I wave him off. "I've heard your explanations and I still think it's B.S. What's more, I think maybe you're trapped by this thing. I know my parents are always on me about following through on things.

'*You signed up for these lessons-*' or '*You signed up for this team. You've got to see it through. No quitting!*' Well, I think sometimes the smartest and the bravest thing is to quit."

We stare out at the view for a bit. Then I start up again.

"I have an aunt who's happily married now, but she was in a lousy marriage before that and she's never said this to me directly, but the family story is that she had second thoughts before she got married to that first guy, but she didn't want to call it off. She didn't want to be a quitter."

Some of the trees still have their leaves, but a lot of them don't. I have an itchy spot on the back of my left hand. I look over at Kyle.

"Here's my theory about the car that came so close to you. I think your cousin Jeff was driving that car – maybe with a hat on or something so he wouldn't be recognized and driving somebody else's car. My guess is that if we walk around the River Bend apartments we'll find a black Jeep with a scratch on the front right side."

"Jeff?" he says.

"There's more. My theory is that he was asked to do it by your Mom, who was hoping to scare you out of Deerwalking. She likes to support everything you do but I think she really, really doesn't want you out in the line of fire and so she worked out some kind of plan with your cousin – not to hit you but to scare you."

"I don't know," he says. "That's pretty crazy."

"When my Mom got home from the hospital, your Mom came over. She was upset and apologizing like she thought it was her fault. I've been thinking about that. Why would she think it was her fault?"

He shrugs. "She thinks my lousy grades in Spanish are her fault."

"When I asked to come here today, I knew your folks wouldn't be around. I figured there must be someone in the area connected to your family who's old enough to drive but young enough to do something a little crazy if asked."

"I don't know. What else? You got any other theories?"

"I know a guy who says if you really want to disrupt hunters, the best way to do it is to drive an ATV around in the woods. That's my back-up plan. If you and Brad come out here on Saturday I'm planning to borrow the Fandell's ATV. Maybe I can recruit your cousin to drive it around in your vicinity."

"My vicinity?"

"Yeah. Don't turn off your cell phone."

We continue to look out at the view. I want to keep making my pitch but I don't want to put him on the spot or back him in a corner.

"I'm not asking you to change your mind right now," I say. "I'm just asking you to consider it. OK? Consider it. Can you do that?"

"Yeah, maybe," he says. "I can consider it."

"Protest in the parking lot. Hand out flyers. Sing songs. Just consider staying out of the woods."

The sun is low. It's been a nice, bright day, but these days it's starting to get dark pretty early. Maybe my itchy spot is some kind of new disease.

"Here's how you communicate it. You say the controversy about Deerwalking was becoming a distraction from your real message. That way, you're not backing down. You're focusing on what's most important."

I expect Kyle is going to say something, but he doesn't. He just stares out to the horizon.

"I'm thinking the hard part is going to be Brad," I say. "He's gung-ho, right? It's not enough to change your mind. You'll need to change his mind, too."

"Maybe."

"So here's what I say to you about that. You're a leader. It's what you do. You get people to do things they wouldn't think to do otherwise. It's very cool. But sometimes being a leader means changing a plan. Sometimes being a leader means getting people to not do things."

"We should get back," he says.

"One more thing. I have an extra reason for wanting to make sure nothing happens to you on Saturday. I'm not sure why, but I'm pretty sure that if anything happens to you on Saturday it'll split up my parents. Maybe that seems pretty stupid compared to you being dead, but it means a lot to me."

"Sure. Course it does."

I'm feeling pretty good about getting that all out, even though the last part felt a little cheesy and I'm embarrassed about getting squeaky-voiced talking about my parents. You hang out for an afternoon with a high school kid and you don't want to act like a baby. Kyle walks down the hill ahead of me, which gives me a chance to get my throat clear.

For some reason, at that moment, I come up with the answer to the escalator problem. It can't be "up-up" and "down-down" because then you'd need "up-down" and "down-up" and how would you know which was which? The answer is coming and going - "coming up" is the up escalator from the floor below you and "going up" is the up escalator to the floor above you. Similarly, you'd have "going down" and "coming down."

This makes me feel better. I don't know if I can make anything better in the world, but maybe I can find the right words for some things. Probably my itchy spot is just an itchy spot.

When we get back to the car, I wonder if Kyle will say something to Jeff about my theory, but he doesn't. He just asks him to take us back.

After dinner and after cleaning up after dinner, I tell Dad I want to show him something outside. We put on coats and he follows me out the door. I get into the passenger side off his car. He sits in the driver's seat.

"Are we going somewhere?" he asks.

"No," I say. "This was just the most private place I could think of. I want to ask you about something."

"Shoot."

I thought it would be easier to do this since I had that talk with Kyle. I'm on a roll, right? I'm doing everything. I'm spilling my guts left and right. But it isn't easy.

"That lady who came to the door last night from your work. Is there something up with you and her?"

I don't know if this is too delicate or too crude, but at least it's out there. I hope Dad doesn't hate me for asking. I hope Dad doesn't hate me for having the question at all.

"Deena is a friend from work. Period, full stop. OK?" He looks at me for a minute. "Your Mom could be taken away to another dimension by aliens tomorrow – I would not run away with Deena. Let me show you something."

He pops the trunk and gets out of the car. I meet him back by the truck. He lifts the lid and there's a big plastic bag. He takes it out and holds it open for me to see. Inside is a dark blue article of clothing. I touch it. It has a rough texture.

"What is it?" I ask.

"It's a Kevlar vest. A bullet-proof vest. I knew Deena had one of these because she's mentioned it before. She tends to worry about things. She decided to get one because she was going to volunteer at a soup kitchen in Hartford. This is what's known as 'overkill.' I asked to borrow it because I'm planning to loan it to Kyle. I figure it's the least I can do for him. I had the lousy idea of trying to protect him by generating a media circus, which we didn't do anyway. So anyway-" He looks around. "You want to continue this in the car?"

I'm not sure if that's a question or a suggestion. I say "Yeah," and we get back in the car.

After we shut the doors, he says, "Anyway, I didn't tell Deena what the vest was for and then she knew I was staying home and that something bad happened to your Mom and Deena decided that I must be in trouble with the Mafia."

"Sure," I say. "I can see that." I do a raspy voice: *"You know, Mr. McAlpine, it'd be a shame if anything were to happen to that nice-looking banjo of yours."*

"She was doing something that you and I wouldn't know anything about. She was overthinking."

"The vest was a good idea," I say. I shrug my shoulders. "Two vests would have been a better idea. He was planning to go out in the woods with his friend, Brad."

Dad looks over at me. "Was planning?"

"When we were out in the woods today, he told me he'd consider changing his mind."

"That would be great. Did he say why?"

"I basically begged him to. We were doing the interview and I was being a good, objective journalist and something just snapped. I couldn't do it anymore. I had to stop and plead with him not to go out and risk getting shot."

"And he's going to think about it?"

"Yeah, and I expect he's going to talk to Brad. He says Brad is all gung-ho, so that might be a challenge, but I think maybe Kyle doesn't want Brad to get shot as much as we don't want Kyle to get shot."

"Well, good work – good work! I hope he changes his mind. If you talked him out of this, we all owe you one. What's your salary as Deputy Editor?"

"Nothing."

"We'll double it!"

I actually get some money from the paper, but it's not a salary. Each summer before school starts up, Dad does an accounting of the paper's income and expenses for the past year and declares a profit amount that gets split three ways and put into our college funds. It seems like a lot of money to me, but I suspect it'll pay for about twenty minutes of college.

Dad looks around. "Are we good?"

"One more question," I say. "If Mom were kidnapped by aliens-"

"Oh, let's not think about it, OK? We had a scare this week, but things are going to be OK. Let's just say that – if your Mom gets kidnapped to another dimension – I'm going to have to find a more extreme version of that vest in the trunk and start researching my inter-dimensional travel options."

6. OUR MOTHER'S SPOUSE WHO LIVES IN THE SPHERE OF HOLINESS

I hear Beth singing and playing on the piano in the family room. She can't really play the piano, but she plays around on it. She's singing:

> *Here we go-*
> *Up the road-*
> *To a birthday party!*

I think there's a real tune that goes to those words, but she's making up her own tune. I sit on the couch and watch. I thought I might cramp her style by moving into the family room, but she doesn't seem to mind. The song modulates:

> *Two bits-*
> *Four bits-*
> *Six bits-*
> *A dollar-*
> *My dog has fleas!*

I think the next part is the bridge. It features one black key played over and over again many times in a row. Time for the big finish, I think.

> *Birds do it-*
> *Bees do it-*
> *Even ten or twenty fleas do it-*

Let's do it-
Let's fall in love!

There's a flurry of loud notes like the end of a fireworks display and the song is over. The audience rises to its feet as one and claps as loudly as I can.

"Very nice!" I say. "What do you call it?"

"Bohemian Rhapsody."

I walk over to her. "There's one part I don't understand," I say. "How can ten or twenty fleas fall in love?"

"Hey," she says, "I just sing 'em. I don't understand 'em."

I figure it's now or never. "I was wondering if you wanted to learn how to do the newspaper."

She looks up at the ceiling and bites her lip. "I don't know. Is it hard?"

It's a fair question. "Yes," I say. "It's ridiculously hard. It's practically impossible. It's like trying to lift the whole world."

"Good."

Mrs. Butler answers the door. "Hi," I say. I'm ready to launch into a little speech reminding her of who I am and introducing Beth and asking for a moment of her time, but she waves us in.

"Oh, good," she says. "Come on in!" She turns to Beth. "And you've brought your sister!"

"I'm Beth."

"Yes, I know. I'm Janie." They shake hands. I send Beth a quick, telepathic message: *Don't call her Janie.* Mrs Butler waves us towards the living room. "What can I get you? We have apple cider and also some diet soda."

"I'm good," I say.

"What kind of soda?" asks Beth.

Mrs. Butler's eyes get big, and she leans in towards Beth. "We have diet cola and diet creme soda." She looks around to make sure there aren't any soda thieves nearby. "The creme soda tastes like something you shouldn't be allowed to drink – but it's perfectly OK for you to drink it!"

"I'll have some of that."

"Coming up!" She looks back at me. "Surely I can get you something?"

At this point I figure I have to let her get me something. "I'll have some water, thank you."

Mrs. Butler disappears and Beth and I go into the living room and sit down. I wonder if Beth is getting a misleading look at life as a newspaper reporter. Not everybody is going to invite you in and serve you creme soda.

"I like the doggy on the pillow!" says Beth to Mrs. Butler, who's coming in with our drinks. There's a picture of a collie stitched into one of the pillows on the couch.

"Isn't that the cutest thing? Kyle gave that to me last Christmas." She hands us our drinks and sits with a drink of her own. I think she's drinking diet creme soda. "So, then. How's your Mom?"

"She's good," I say. "Getting better."

"I'm so glad to hear it. Your Mom is the Best! So, is this a newspaper call? If you're here for Kyle, I'm afraid he's over at a friend's house right now."

Brad Desjardins, I think. *He's over at Brad's house.*

"Yes," I say, "this is a newspaper call. In fact, it's Beth's first newspaper call."

"We're honored," she says to Beth. "And not the last, I'm sure!"

I pull out a notepad and my pod. "Can you tell us what Kyle's plans are for Saturday?"

She looks back at me and reorients herself to be facing halfway between us. I feel like Mrs. Butler would rather be having a diet creme soda tea party with Beth. Still, she seems happy. I take that as a good sign.

"I can't talk for Kyle, of course. Kyle's spoken for himself since – well, pretty much since he could talk. But I don't think I'm telling tales out of school to let you know that he's been seriously rethinking his plans. And – just as a side note – let me say that I think this shows tremendous maturity on his part. When you draw a line in the sand and say, *'I'm going to do x, y, or z'* - it's very hard to change your mind. If I say I'm going to do something, I want to do it – even if it doesn't seem like a good idea anymore. But what he realized – and this is what I think is so adult, so beyond his years. In fact, I think it's something a lot of grown-ups wouldn't be able to figure out. What he realized was that this Deerwalking business was becoming a distraction from the real message he's been trying to get across. And what's really important to him is the message."

Beth gives her a big grin. "This soda is good!"

"I'm glad you like it, Sweetie!"

I write "MIGHT CHANGE PLANS - DISTRACTION" in my notepad. I'm thinking that she's wrong about what Kyle's possible change of heart says about him. If he's coming to his senses, it's not that he's zooming forward to adulthood. He's regressing. He's drifting back to the good sense he had before he was a teenager.

"So," I say, "Kyle's thinking about changing his plans, but you can't say anything definite at this time?"

"Yes, I think that's right."

"And what about his friend, Brad, or anyone else who was planning to go Deerwalking, too? If Kyle changes his mind, will they go without him?"

"That'd be a good question for Kyle. I think the others look to him as a leader, so I'd hope they'd join him in whatever the new plan is."

"What's the doggy's name?" This is Beth, pointing to the pillow.

"Excuse me?"

Beth picks up the pillow and points to the dog. "The doggy on the pillow. What's his name?"

It's funny, but I feel like Beth and I are finding a rhythm together. It's not quite a good cop – bad cop routine. It's more like having a cop interview you while there's a TV on in the background tuned to a cartoon show.

"I don't know that we've ever given that dog a name. It's not a picture of a real dog as far as I know. It's just a picture. Still – why not give him a name? Right?" She looks at me and back at Beth. "His name is Thumper."

I write "THUMPER," but I'm not sure why. She just made it up. And wasn't Thumper the name of a rabbit? I hesitate, then tell myself: *You're never going to get the answers to the questions you don't ask.*

"My Dad borrowed a bullet-proof vest that he was planning to loan to Kyle, if he wants it, to help keep him a little safer on Saturday. He did this thinking that Kyle was going to be out Deerwalking. Should I tell him to forget it?"

This seems to have some effect on Mrs. Butler. She smiles at Beth and looks at me and then smiles again at Beth and then looks at me. "That's very interesting. I'm very grateful for the thought," she says, but her throat closes up on "thought" and she has to stop. We wait. She takes a sip of her soda. "Anyway, I don't think Kyle's going to need it, but maybe he'll know someone who could use it."

Beth looks up from the pillow. "A bullet-proof vest?" she says. "Is that like magic?"

I'm not sure if she's asking me or Mrs. Butler.

"I don't know anything about it," says Mrs. Butler. "I didn't know it was something you could go out and get."

She looks a little sick, like maybe she's imagining finding out about bullet-proof vests after Kyle had gotten shot.

"It's not magic," I say. "It doesn't stop everything – and if you put one on there's still plenty of you that can get shot."

Beth looks at Mrs. Butler. "Did you know my folks when they were kids?"

She smiles. "I knew your Dad when we were both in high school in West Hartford. I met your Mom when she was engaged to your Dad."

This is news to me. I think of Mrs. Butler as Mom's friend, but apparently she was Dad's friend first. Also, I think of Mrs. Butler as older than Mom and Dad because Kyle is older than Brian, but I guess they're about the same age. A little voice in the back of my head says: *What if Dad is Kyle's father?*

This would explain a few things, like Dad borrowing the vest and Mom and Dad arguing at night and Mrs. Butler's complicated-seeming relationship with Mom. I wonder if everybody but us knows that our Dad is Kyle's father. That would be pretty weird. The neighborhood reporters are oblivious to something in their own family that everybody else in the neighborhood knows about. Or maybe Brian and Beth know about it, too, and it's just me who's clueless.

Still, it doesn't seem very likely. Does Kyle look like Dad? I'm not sure. Also, I don't think you need to be related to somebody in order to worry about their safety. I've been worried about Kyle's safety and I didn't think he was my brother. I should stop pairing up my Dad in my head with other women. Don't think about a white gorilla.

Mrs. Butler tilts her head and lifts her eyebrows. "Can you guys keep a secret?"

"Sure!" says Beth.

Mrs. Butler leans in. "I think I know what I'll get Kyle for Christmas this year. One of those vests! I don't care if it isn't perfect. I'd still be happy to have him wear it to school every day." She takes a swig of creme soda and looks at the ceiling. "Maybe I could get one embroidered with a picture of Thumper!"

I'm the teacher and Beth's the student. I know I'm talking too much but I'm hoping she'll learn something anyway.

"There are two key parts to being a reporter. Part One is getting the story – the information for the story. Part Two is writing it up. Getting the story means going around and asking questions and taking notes. I'm pretty sure you can do that already. You know about a lot of stuff before I do. Part Two – writing it up – takes practice.

"Dad does an exercise with us sometimes called the Five Changes. He'll give us a sentence or a poem or something and have us rewrite it five times – one time with no a's – one time with no e's – that's a hard one – then no i's and no o's and no u's. So you have to find five pretty different ways to say the same thing.

"And when you first try it, it seems pretty impossible and also like it has nothing to do with writing an article for the paper. It just seems like this crazy puzzle to solve. But after a while, there's a kind of power to it. You start to see that there are always lots of different ways you can say the same thing, and it's good to have choices.

"So let's try one together. We'll take the start of the Lord's Prayer. Let's write it down:

> *Our Father who art in Heaven*

"Let's start with the no-u version. What needs to change? Right. The 'Our'. Can we say 'Yours and my Father'? No, that's still got a u. How about 'The Father of You and Me'? Still doesn't work, right? What might work? Any ideas? Here are some possibilities:

> *Everyone's Father who art in Heaven*
> *The Father of All who art in Heaven*
> *Father in Heaven*

"Actually, *Father in Heaven* would work for the no-o version as well. For the no-i version, we need to find a way to get rid of the "in." But you can't say:

> *Our Father who art Heaven*

"That wouldn't make sense. You could say:

> *Our Father who lives in Heaven*

178

"But now we have two i's instead of one. Sometimes, the best way to get rid of a word is to rearrange things:

Our Heavenly Father

"The no-e version means we need to do without Father or Heaven. So we have to find other words or phrases that will get the idea across:

Our Dear Holy God
Holy King of Our World's Family

"And that leaves the no-a version. Again, we can't have Father or Heaven. But the no-e versions won't work, either. We need to find some other combinations:

Our Wonderful Holy God
Holy King of Our World's People
Our Mother's Spouse who lives in the Sphere of Holiness

"I'm not saying that's a good example. I just want you to get the idea because this is actually a homework assignment. Here's the phrase:

My dog has fleas.

"I want you to do the Five Changes on 'My dog has fleas'. Can you do that?"

Beth stares at the words I've written down. "Maybe," she says. "What's the dog's name?"

I'm reading in bed. Gollum is supposed to be leading Sam and Frodo to Mordor, although you never know with Gollum. Dad looks in.

"Hey."

I look up. "Hey."

"I just talked to your buddy, Kyle Butler. He says he doesn't need the vest on Saturday. He says I should tell you that they decided that the Deerwalking stuff was becoming a distraction from their message. So he and Brad and some others are planning to set up an information table in the state forest parking lot Saturday morning. He says that I should put the vest on you and bring you to see their table. What do you think?"

"Let's do it."

"They're going to be there starting at five in the morning."

I put a marker in the book. "I don't think we need to be there right when they start."

"Good."

Being a Deputy Editor is sort of like being a drummer or a punter. It's not something you can do by yourself. You need to be part of a team. They say if you take an ant away from its colony and give it a nice place to live with plenty of food and water it just dies. An ant is a little Deputy Editor. Or another way of looking at it is that I'm a big version of an ant. I go out from my colony and into the world and bring stuff back. Out and back, out and back. I'm kind of small, but I'm more powerful that you'd think. Mom says that if an ant was human-sized it could pick up a train car.

So what can I do about the paper? It seems like a longshot that Beth can just take over for Brian. I don't know if Mom would even let her do rounds. I did the whole neighborhood once when Brian was sick and it took me all day. I don't want to do that over and over. Maybe Mr. Patel was right all along. The problem with the newspaper is that it isn't scalable.

What else could I do? I could play the drums or start punting. Maybe I could play the banjo. Apparently you can do that on your own if you know enough songs and some jokes. I could see Brian doing that. Given that I suck at Name That Tune I'm probably not going to get very far as a musician. Given my size, I'm probably not going to get very far as a football player, either.

"Phone's for you," says Beth. She hands me something, a folded-up piece of paper, and I go into the kitchen and pick up the phone.

"Hi! It's me." It's Lucille.

"Hi," I say.

"How you doing tonight?"

"I'm good."

"My friend Charlene got punched in the eye. It was all red and swollen."

"Oh." I don't want to keep the conversation going, but now I'm curious. "Who punched her?"

"Exactly! Who punched her? She says it was a robber behind the school who wanted to steal her backpack, but she didn't report it to the school. I think it was somebody else."

I want to figure this out. I want to ask a hundred questions and draw a map and figure out who punched Charlene and then write an article about it. I wonder if there's any way I can do this without talking to Lucille.

I unfold the paper in my hand.

> *MY DOG HAS FLEAS*
> *5 CHANGES*
> *BY ELIZABETH MCALPINE*
>
> *NO U - MY DOG HAS FLEAS. (EASY!)*
> *NO I - MY DOG HAS FLEAS. (EASY!)*
> *NO O - MY PUPPY HAS FLEAS.*
> *NO E - MY DOG HAS BUGS.*
> *NO A - MY DOG IS INFESTED WITH LITTLE CREEPY THINGS. (D*D HELPED)*
>
> *P.S. IT'S JUST MADE UP. NO FLEAS ON JOHANN THE WONDER DOG!*

Lucille's changed the subject. "They're having a dance at my school on the 24th. I think that's two weeks from tonight. You want to come?"

I'm encouraged by Beth's playfulness. I think D*D is Dad and she didn't want to write the A on the no-A line. I set down the paper and try to focus. "No, thank you, Lucille. You're nice and I wish you well and I wouldn't mind helping you figure out who punched your friend, but I'm not your boyfriend and I'm not going to a dance at your school. And there's a call I need to make now, so I'm going to say Good Night. Be well. OK?"

"OK, Darren. Good night."

I hang up the phone and find Beth in her room.

"Hey," I say.

"Hey."

"Good job on the Changes."

"Thanks. Dad helped with the A."

"That's OK. That's good, even. When you're a reporter, you shouldn't try to do everything yourself. Speaking of which, I have something I want to ask you about."

"OK."

"I'm thinking I shouldn't just talk on the phone to Lucille or any other girl I don't really want to talk to. I should talk to a girl I want to talk to."

"Megan?"

"No, not Megan. She's too old for me. I want to talk to a girl in my own class. What I'm wondering is what I should say."

"You want to put out a feeler? Is that it?"

"I guess so."

"And she's in a class with you?"

"Yes."

"What you do is you call her up and ask about a homework assignment. *'I lost my notebook. What was the assignment?' 'I lost the handout. Can you make me a copy?'* Something like that."

"And that's putting out a feeler?"

"Oh, yes. She'll see right through you. And if she wants to talk with you she will and if she doesn't she won't."

"Thanks."

I go back to my room and find my math homework and a class list then I go back to the kitchen and dial.

"Hello?" It's a man's voice.

"Hello. This is Darren McAlpine. Is Becca there?"

"Just a sec."

I hear some muffled talking in the background. I can't make out the words, so I try to feel the meaning.

- *Who is this jerk, calling you at home?*

- *Nobody. He's a complete nobody. I'll get rid of him in a minute.*

"Hello?"

"Hi, Becca. This is Darren from math class." I pause to see if she's willing to acknowledge knowing me. It's a long moment.

"Sure. What's up?"

"Something happened to my notes from today. I was wondering if you could tell me what our homework is."

"Sure. Just give me a sec."

There's a clunk and then some background noise and a hushed exchange I can't quite catch.

- *So, when's the wedding?*

- *In his dreams!*

- *Don't talk to him or he'll think you like him.*

"Hi, Darren? Do you have something to write with?"

"Yes."

"Chapter Three-dash-Two. Even problems two to fourteen."

"Good. Thanks. Anything else?"

"She says *'Show your work'.*"

"Yeah. I could probably guess that part. I feel like I should show my work when I fill in my name and the date at the top of the paper."

She laughs, for which I'm very grateful. "How would you do that?"

"I don't know. For my name, maybe I equals me through the transitive property. For the date, take yesterday's date and add one."

"You actually understand this stuff, don't you? I'm thinking this may be my one chance ever to help you with math homework."

"A lot of it makes sense to me. Some parts don't. I think Mrs. Featherstone makes it harder than it needs to be."

I can't think of what else to say but don't want to hang up. Dead air. Maybe she'll hang up. I feel like I'm holding a seashell up to my ear. I can hear the ocean.

"Did you hear that Bobby Dugan is moving?" she says.

"No."

"His family's going to Florida. I think next week is his last week."

"I didn't know that. Is he looking forward to it or is he bummed?"

"I'm not sure. I think a little of both."

We wait, but nothing else happens.

"Well," I say, "thanks for the assignment."

"Sure."

"See you Monday."

"Bye."

I hang up. I equals me is actually the reflexive property. I used to know this stuff. Maybe I'm slipping already.

Oh well. She had her chance to hang up and instead told me that Bobby Dugan is moving. And Yes, it's possible that this was on her mind because she's in love with him and all she can think about night and day is Bobby Dugan. But I could live with that. He's moving to Florida in a week and will be safely out of the picture.

Maybe I could do a smaller paper just for my current route:

ETA
The Eastern Thomson Acres
Enquirer Tribune Advocate

GST
Glenbrook, Springbrook and Thomson
Gazette Star Tribune

TAE
Thomson Acres - East
Tribune Advocate Enquirer

TANG
Thomson Acres No-Pee Gazette.

As Dad and I are pulling up into a parking spot, we can see a couple of hunters talking to Kyle and Brad. I get out my pod. Kyle and Brad are standing at a long table. The hunters – they have to be hunters – are two men wearing bright orange vests over camo jackets. This seems a little funny to me. Why put on a camouflage jacket and then put on a bright orange vest? Do you want to blend in or do you want to stand out?

I take a couple of pictures of the scene. One of the men is pointing to a sign on a stick at the corner of the table that says "DEER HUNTING INFORMATION". Kyle's handouts were probably not the kind of Deer Hunting Information this guy was expecting. He waves his hands like he's trying to shoo Kyle and Brad away and then both hunters head off together.

Dad and I walk up to the table.

"Hey," says Dad. "We understand this is a good place to get deer hunting information!"

"We need to change the sign," says Kyle. "I feel bad. I wasn't trying to trick anybody. We have all this information about deer hunting, right? So I just wrote "deer hunting information" on the sign. So everybody who walks up to us thinks we can tell them the best places to go to bag a deer."

185

"Maybe we just take the sign down," says Brad.

"Yeah, I guess maybe so," says Kyle. "We'd be better off with a sign that says 'We Hate Hunters'. Nobody would stop, but at least if anybody did stop they wouldn't feel like we were trying to trick them." He points at me. "You could've figured this out, right? I should've checked with you about the sign."

"Maybe," I say.

"You wearing the vest?" I open my jacket so he can see the bullet-proof vest I'm wearing under it. "Good. Come over here. I want to show you something."

I follow him over to some parked cars. He looks back at the others and speaks quietly. "Actually, I just wanted to tell you that I found the car. You were right. A black Jeep with a scratch by the right headlight at the River Bend parking lot. I stood up by the corner of it and got a flashback. Anyway, I'm sorry your Mom got hurt just because my family members can't talk to me straight."

I'm not sure what to say to this. You can't say: 'That's OK. I don't mind that my Mom got hurt.'

"Families," I say. "What are you going to do?"

Dad and Brad are doing something with the sign on the table. I think they're taking it down. Could I have helped him word it better? Probably. It's just copy editing.

"So," I say, "are you going to say anything to your cousin or your Mom?"

"I'm going to say something to my Mom. I've got to. She's my Mom."

"Yeah."

He looks at the sign coming down and then back at me. "Anything else I should know about?"

I don't think I have anything else, but then I do. I keep my voice down. "Want to know what you're going to get for Christmas?"

Bye-week Saturdays seem like holidays to me. You can take a trip up to the state forest parking lot and still have time for a long, lazy morning. It's always good to have a day off as long as you have something to go back to.

Something catches my eye in the backyard. I go out and take a look. It's a brand new football. I pick it up. There's a sticker on it listing its features. It has a new football smell. I throw it up in the air a few times. It feels pretty good. I peel off the sticker and put the sticker in my pocket and take the football to the sports box in the garage.

I think: *OK, Mr. Johnson. Now we're square.*

It would have been nice if he'd put a card or a note on it. Probably he was afraid of getting something wrong. What's the worst that could have happened? Maybe I'd have thrown his note back over the fence with blue circles around the unclear antecedents.

"Call for you," says Brian. I hurry to the phone. Maybe Becca is calling me back.

"Hello?"

"Hey! Connor here."

"Oh. Hi." I've never gotten a call from Connor. "What's up?"

"Here's the deal. My Dad says I have to find a job or I'm, like, dead, you know? So what can I do, right? So I'm trying to think what I could do and I think of your paper, right? It would be totally boss if I could help out with your paper. Like I could go door to door up whatever streets you wanted. Something like that."

"Oh." I don't know if this is a good idea or a terrible idea. I need some time to think about it. "That's an interesting idea."

"I can start like anytime and I don't need to earn a lot of money. I just need to be able say I'm working, OK?"

"I need to talk to my Dad and my brother."

"OK."

"I'll call you back."

"OK."

"Probably not today. It could take me a couple of days to get you an answer."

"OK."

I think about saying something rude or ridiculous to see if he'd say OK, but I just say Good Bye and hang up.

Good idea or a terrible idea? I'm not sure. Connor is a little crazy and I'm not sure he can write at all. On the other hand, he's outgoing and would do fine going door to door. It's a tough call. He might be president someday but I don't know if he's cut out to be a newspaper boy.

Beth's chore this week is cleaning the garage. I look in on her and she's sweeping up a storm. She's very industrious when she's asked to do something specific. She sees me but doesn't stop sweeping.

"I had a thought," I say.

"What?" She's still sweeping.

"I thought you might try writing a column for the newspaper about neighborhood rumors."

She stops. The garage is foggy with dust.

"Rumors?"

"Sure," I say. "You know, nothing bad. Nothing we can't print. Just stuff you've heard about. Somebody's going to move. Somebody's going to change schools. Somebody's getting married."

"What does a column mean?"

"It means we'd try to make it a regular feature every time we do a paper, like Brian's sports round-up."

"Would I have to write it with no e's or something?"

"No. Just write it. I'm thinking a three-dot column. What that means is that you write a sentence about something and then you put three dots and then you write a sentence about something else. And you do that five or ten times and that's the column. The other rule is that when you mention anybody's name you put it in bold letters. Think you can do that?"

She gives me a look. "Maybe." She picks up the broom. "Maybe Mr. SpongeBob Bossypants. Maybe I'll put in four dots."

"Sounds good," I say. "Might be a record."

"How will I know the rumors?"

"I don't know. Ask around. Seems like you know a lot of stuff already."

"What about my dolls and stuffed animals?"

"What about them?"

"I know all their rumors. Can I put those in the column?"

"Maybe. Maybe Mrs. SpongeBob Bossypants. But maybe you shouldn't put more than one item in any one column about your dolls or stuffed animals."

She starts sweeping again. "I'll think about it," she says. "Maybe I'll write some rumors about you."

Today at church is Stewardship Sunday. There's a Stewardship Sermon by the Stewardship Chair. If the sermon is a drinking game, the word is "stewardship". Sometimes it means giving to the church and sometimes it means being responsible and not wasting things. At least that's how I understand him when he makes a transition from stewardship of our money to stewardship of the Earth. I don't think he means that we should pledge a portion of the Earth to the church. Then he talks for a while about stewardship of our time, which could be either kind.

He says: "I'd like to turn now to stewardship of talent. This is a very important kind of stewardship. Some of us live in denial about this, but don't kid yourself. We all have talents. You have talents. Don't deny them. Find constructive ways to use them. Use them in church. Use them outside of church. Make the world a better place. That's stewardship of your talents."

Then he comes back to money and I tune out because I don't really have any money. But I do have a few odd talents, and I think a lot about how to figure out how to use them. I wish he'd been a little more specific about how you do that. It isn't usually obvious, at least to me. Figuring this out is kind of my job at this point.

Some people's talents are right there on the surface for everybody to see. That doesn't make them better talents, but it probably makes them easier talents to live with. Some talents are less obvious. You go to a football game and you notice the quarterback and maybe a couple of other players. You don't notice the little guy sitting on the bench in the clean uniform. Why is he even there? But in the last minute, when the game is on the line, they send in the little guy and it turns out he can kick a football in a high, straight, forty-yard arc and win the game.

That's a metaphor. I can't kick a football in a high, straight arc across my backyard.

Here's another metaphor. I wear my talents under my shirt on a chain around my neck. There's a mysterious power in them that binds me in a fellowship and propels me towards Mordor.

"I'll make you a deal," says Beth.

"OK. What?"

"I'll write that rumor column, but you need to help me with the wedding today."

"Wedding?"

"Yes, wedding! Hello? Miss Squirrel and Mr. Bear – right? You know this – right?"

"Oh, right. I do know this." I think about saying something bogus like I thought they might call it off or elope. She's looking at me. "All right," I say. "Let's do it."

Beth leads me to the family room, where the chair and sofa cushions have been arranged into a canyon of matrimony. The business end of the canyon is identified by a wooden box of coasters, looking surprisingly altar-like. Barbie is resting nearby. I wonder if she's going to officiate.

Beth turns to me. "I need to get Miss Squirrel ready. You fix up the altar and make sure Mr. Bear is ready."

"Got it," I say. "How long until the wedding starts?"

"Ten minutes."

She head off to her room. I don't see Miss Squirrel. I guess she's waiting in Beth's room. I believe it's unlucky for the squirrel to be seen by the bear before the wedding.

Mr. Bear doesn't need a lot of help to look ready for a wedding. He has a bow tie permanently attached to the front of his neck. I decide the altar needs a cloth. There's a square of lacy material on one of the end tables. It fits just right side to side, although it runs onto the floor at the front and back of the altar.

Mom is cooking in the kitchen. She still has a big bandage, but is looking better. She's chopping vegetables but stops when I stand looking at her.

"I'm helping Beth with the wedding."

"That's nice!"

"Do we have any little birthday candles? I promise not to light them."

Mom puts down the knife and digs in around in a drawer. "For a cake?" she asks, as she pulls out a package and holds out a handful of birthday candles in different colors. I take two white candles with spiral blue stripes.

"For the altar. Thanks!" I head off.

"How're you going to get them to stand up?"

I stop and turn around. "An excellent question. How am I going to get them to stand up?"

"You're going to use little lumps of Play-Doh. Oldest trick in the book. What are they going on top of?"

"The coaster box with that blue, lacy square on top."

"Hold on." She opens another drawer and does some pulling and ripping and holds something out for me. "Second oldest trick in the book. For under the Play-Doh."

I go back and she hands me two little squares of waxed paper. "Got it. Thanks again!"

I use little blue lumps of Play-Doh to hold the candles. We've got a color scheme going here. Still no Beth or Miss Squirrel, so I duck out to the backyard. You'd think nothing would be growing this time of year, but there's a little yellow dandelion flower in the lawn. I pluck the stem and bring it in. There's no way to make the stem work. I take the stem off and set the head of the flower on the altar between the two candles. Darren McAlpine: church flower lady of family room pretend weddings.

Beth comes in, carrying the bride, who is wearing a gauzy white dress with a long train that I suspect has depleted Mom's medical supplies. I get the groom into position and Beth sings the organ part:

> *Here comes Miss Squirrel!*
> *Here comes Miss Squirrel!*
> *Here comes, here comes, here comes Miss Squirrel!*

When the bride gets to the front, Beth takes the groom from me and has them face one another. She looks at me and nods towards the Barbie doll. I move the doll into position. Beth had better be a really good columnist.

I speak for Barbie. "Dearly beloved, we are gathered here today to celebrate the marriage of Mr. Bear to the very beautiful Miss Squirrel. And I know what I'm talking about. This is the Reverend Barbie speaking. I know from beautiful. Now then: Is there anyone here who knows any reason why this bear and this squirrel cannot be married today? Speak now or forever hold your peace."

We wait a moment. Nobody objects.

"So. Mr. Bear..."

"Darren," says Beth.

"What?"

"Mr. Bear's first name is Darren."

"So. Darren. Do you take Miss Squirrel?"

"What's her name?"

I look at Beth. "You tell me."

"No," she says. "You tell me. I thought her name was Megan, but I think I was wrong."

That stinker, Beth! I'm thinking she just wants me to join her in playing with her dolls for a while, but she wants more. Lucky for her I'm in a generous mood.

"Darren Bear, do you take Becca Squirrel to be your wife in sickness and health so long as you live?"

Mr. Bear nods vigorously and says "I do!"

"Becca Squirrel, do you take Darren Bear to be your husband in sickness and health so long as you live?"

Miss Squirrel nods. "I do!"

"By the power vested in me, I now declare you Bear and Squirrel."

The newlyweds mash their faces together for quite a while.

"What happens now?" I ask.

Beth gives me a look like it's a dumb question. "We write it up for the paper," she says.

Brian gives a shout that it's time for dinner. Beth settles the couple into the honeymoon box and heads to the table. I take a detour to the bathroom.

I'm up on the hill in the state forest, looking out over the woods and the reservoir. Actually, I'm up over the hill. I'm a good fifty feet off the ground. This is higher than I can normally levitate on my own. My arms are full of something that pulls me up like a helium balloon. It's thousands of little birds. Why don't they get crushed? When I shift my weight, some of the birds come loose. When they leave my arms, they turn into flower petals and flutter slowly down. It's a magic trick. I drift on the wind down towards Thomson Acres. I drift out to the end of Springbrook and then turn around so that I can do my route from above. I'm a holy salt shaker. Over every house I shake loose some birds that turn into flower petals. Petals for you, DiFurias and your maybe-baby. Petals for you, Carlsens. Take good care of that dog or Mrs. Waldron will get it! Petals for you, nice old Mrs. Everett. No flood to wipe you out today – just a soft rain of rose petals. Petals for Bumgarners and Fandalls and Mrs. Luebker and everyone on Springbrook and Thomson and Glenbrook. Petals for home. Plenty of petals to make it look like we got snowed on. Should I come down and land? It might be nice to land, but it seems like it would be small-minded somehow. I should keep going. I'm a holy salt shaker and I still have big armfuls of magic birds.

Made in the USA
Las Vegas, NV
09 February 2021